THE WAKING

Cheryl McClamrock

KW
Kingdom Winds
Publishing

First Edition, 2020
ISBN 13: 978-1-64590-014-6

Published by Kingdom Winds Publishing.
www.kingdomwinds.com
publishing@kingdomwinds.com

Printed in the United States of America.

This book is dedicated to my husband and three boys. They watched as I spent countless hours writing and wrestling over what you now hold in your hands. Their encouragement was always with me reminding me that I would complete this project and that it would be great. And to God my Savior who gave me both the dreams and fire to write what He put in my heart. To Him be the glory.

PROLOGUE

Amora sat up, gasping, a scream caught in her throat. Her eyes scanned the dark room. The familiar shapes of furniture and her sleeping sisters' forms came into focus; the fear began to wane. Her breathing slowed, and she swung her legs over the side of the small cot. She sat for a moment, listening to the room and beyond it to the shadows.

"Did you have another nightmare?" whispered Anna, still facing the wall in the cot across from Amora's.

Her little sister's slight form barely created a bump under the thin sheet. Amora winced as her feet touched the cold stone floor. She tip-toed a couple of steps to her sister's cot and sat on the edge. Anna shifted to her back, and Amora stroked the side of her sister's nine-year-old face. "You haven't slept tonight."

"You know I'd rather be awake when they come for us."

"Anna, they don't come every night."

Amora's eyes darted to the bedroom door locked from the outside. She looked back into her sister's dark-circled eyes. "You need to sleep. If you continue to nod off during training, it will be worse for you."

"I can't. I try, but I'm too afraid. Being pulled out of sleep feels like waking up into a nightmare I can't get free of." Amora was silent for a moment. Anna reached for her hand. "What was the dream? What did you see this time?"

Amora hesitated.

"Tell me."

Amora crossed her arms and looked over at the sleeping form of Alanna, their six-year-old baby sister. Amora turned back to Anna, dropping her voice.

"I saw a woman with dark hair, dressed in leather armor. She came to take me away from here. And then I saw death. Giants, monsters, and other terrible creatures were coming through portals and killing everyone in their path. There was blood, people screaming, and fires burning everywhere."

"Did the woman get us too?"

Amora had a knot in her chest. "Anna, it was just a dream." She turned away from her sister.

"Your dreams are never just dreams, Amora."

Suddenly, the bedroom door crashed open, a deafening sound breaking through the quiet of the night. Three black-robed men strode in with violent purpose. Little

Alanna, waking abruptly from a sound sleep, sat up and screamed. One of the men, the largest, who had a blonde beard, backhanded her roughly, and she began to cry and scream even louder. The man balled his fist and moved toward the little girl again.

Anna, eyes wide with terror, clenched her thin sheet and pressed her back to the wall. Hearing her sister's screams and seeing him go toward her again, Amora's fear turned to unbridled rage. She felt a familiar switch flip inside her mind as something primal took over. She lunged for the man. Her small fists crashed into his stomach with a strength and speed that he was unprepared for. The impact immediately emptied his lungs, and he yelped as his back slammed into the wall. He collapsed to the floor, coughing and retching, as the other two men quickly jumped on Amora, taking her to the ground.

Her head slammed against the hard floor, and she blacked out.

CHAPTER 1

Gianna's eyes opened to the sound of running water. *Did I leave the bathtub on?*

She sat up quickly at the thought, heart pounding in panic. *"Huh? What the —?"*

She shielded her eyes with her hand as she fought to adjust them to the brightness of her surroundings.

Am I dreaming?

All around her were walls of high, green hedges that went on and on as far as she could see. *More likely losing my mind from the extreme stress I've been under lately. What am I lying on? Concrete?* She looked down to see she was on a stone bench. Gianna ran her fingers along its smooth, cool surface. She reached up and laid her hand on her chest.

Is this leather? Oh my God, this is so bizarre!

Gianna felt panic rise in her chest. *What is going on?* Where her red, flannel pajamas had been, now she wore black, leather pants. Her top was also black leather but made of coarser material than the pants. It was stiff and had buckles with leather straps. She couldn't see the back

1

but felt the straps at her shoulders crisscross as they went behind her.

Her upper arms and upper back were left bare, revealing a cross and flame tattoo on her left shoulder blade. Hardened leather guards were secured to her wrists and forearms, and her long brown hair was braided down her back. She was also clad in black knee-high, military boots.

These are awesome. I bet I look amazing in this outfit.

Gianna smiled and wondered if marathon-watching Marvel movies had prompted this dream.

This feels so real, though.

She noticed a set of short swords next to her on the bench that surely hadn't been there a second ago. She'd seen similar blades before in martial arts movies and immediately knew that they were sais.

Ha! At least my geekiness is good for something!

Gianna admired the beauty of the ornately decorated handles, which fit perfectly in her hands, and noted how the shiny metal glinted in the sunlight. She stood up, holding the weapons, and began to wonder if she had any skills with them. If it was a dream, she could probably do whatever she wanted in it.

The Waking

She walked toward a large, green hedge wall in front of her, slashed at it, and found that without thought or much effort, the blades spun smoothly in her hands. Gianna then turned and slashed another bush. "Hi-Yah!"

She also figured that's the typical sound one should make when using martial arts weaponry. Curious, she bounded down the path, performed two summer-sault kicks in the air, and came down with a slicing, "Yaah!" She raised her eyebrows and grinned, "Woh!" She was almost giddy, wondering what else she was capable of here.

Suddenly, a hissing sound startled Gianna into a fighting stance. She turned quickly and caught her breath. An immense, black, snake-like beast writhed around the shoulders, neck, and head of a large angel statue at the end of the hedge wall. The marble warrior's wings extended behind it, with its sword lifted as if about to strike. The serpentine creature it wore had its red eyes fixed on Gianna, and its dragon-like mouth gaped wide, revealing large fangs dripping with venom. It hissed and beat its large, leathery wings in warning.

Still in a fighting stance and afraid to move, Gianna's heart beat loudly in her ears as she weighed her chances of escape if she ran. She gripped her blades, pointed one towards the beast, and glared at the monster. "I'm not afraid! This is my dream, and I'm going to win!"

Suddenly, a tingling sensation in her shoulders traveled down her arms to her hands and fingers. Gianna threw the first blade, and it struck the beast through a wing, pinning it to the statue's chest.

It immediately let out a hair-raising screech, its thick body lashing about as it tried to free itself from the statue. As it continued to snap its horrible jaws at her, the tingling sensation turned to heat in Gianna's left arm. She threw the second blade, and it struck the creature through the right eye. After one final screech, the beast hung limply from the statue's chest still pinned by the wing.

Gianna breathed deeply, rubbing her shoulders as she quickly scanned the area for any other unpleasant surprises. "Okay, that was pretty serious. Cool, but serious. What could be happening to me?"

She put her hands on her hips, replaying the events from the previous night. She had laid down, cried like usual...then nothing. Panic seized her heart. Had she been drugged and kidnapped? "That still wouldn't explain the martial arts," she murmured aloud. She walked back towards the statue to retrieve her weapons. "Huh?"

The creature's body was gone. Gianna turned quickly in every direction, afraid it would pounce on her at any moment...but nothing. One blade remained in the angel's chest, where the creature had been just moments before; the other lay on the ground at its feet. She whispered, "Curiouser and curiouser . . ." as she picked up the sai and placed it in her belt. She struggled to get the other blade free from the statue. After a yank, it suddenly came loose, causing her to land hard on her rear, knocking the wind out of her. She sat stunned for a moment.

Okay. This does not feel like a dream. Maybe I got sucked through a portal? I'm in Wonderland? Narnia? Oz?

"Alice didn't get fighting gear and powers, though," she said out loud. "Lord, what is happening to me? Have I been kidnapped and brainwashed? Maybe I'm strapped to a table in a lab right now..."

Once again, Gianna noticed the sound of water – the same sound she had woken up to. It seemed close by. She felt a strong need to find the water source, so she set about looking for a way to it. She was puzzled about how to locate an opening in the hedgerow or just to make one. Looking ahead, she saw only yards of green walls on both sides. She decided to jog through and see if she could get somewhere. As she ran, which was amazingly easy, the hedges began to blur, and Gianna realized she could run extremely fast. It felt like she could run for hours without getting winded or breaking a sweat. Then, suddenly, she was at a dead end. She attempted to stop abruptly and stumbled into the bush ahead. "Where in the world did that come from?" Gianna freed herself from the leaves. As she looked up, there was the opening she had been hoping for. She stared mouth agape at the sound's source: a massive, five-tiered, white stone fountain.

It was located in the middle of an immense courtyard, spewing the water out tall, grand, and powerful before it fell and poured down the tiers. As the water streamed down, the churning mist formed hundreds of tiny rainbows in the moist air. Gianna walked into the mist, shut her eyes, and stood, arms splayed like a kid in a summer rain shower, as the spray covered her skin. She spun and indulged in the remarkable feelings that the fountain shower seemed to awaken in her senses.

"Um… Excuse me, Miss."

Gianna's eyes popped open, startled. A pretty, young Hispanic girl stood in front of her, probably no older than sixteen. She had short, black hair, and a long, grey cloak draped across her small-framed shoulders. She was wearing a black top, leather pants, and boots similar to what Gianna was wearing, but she had no weapons. Her big, brown eyes made Gianna think of her young son, Dylan.

"S—Sorry. I hope I didn't disturb you, Miss, but are you from this place? Can you tell me how to get outta' here?"

Gianna's motherly instincts kicked in and she reached to put a hand on the young girl's shoulder. "No, sorry, sweetie. I'm not from here and don't know how to get out or how I got here, for that matter."

The girl smiled. "Hey, I'm Luciana, but everyone calls me Lucy."

"Lucy, I'm Gianna. And I'm so glad to meet you and know I'm not the only one who woke up in this weird place." They moved away from the fountain and looked at the tree-encircled courtyard. "I'm sure we can figure out what's happening. We found each other here, maybe someone else will come along."

Lucy's eyes got big, and she grinned. "You woke up here too? All I know is, I went to sleep like normal, and then I woke up in this place, dressed like I'm an extra in the Lord of the Rings movies!" She giggled and held out the ends of her gray cloak. "I think I'm dreaming, only it feels real. Like, I feel this wet mist all over me; I can even taste it."

Gianna nodded, still enjoying the feeling of the mist. Meanwhile, Lucy's face quickly turned serious.

"Miss Gianna, there's something else that's crazy." She stepped closer and whispered, "I have superhero powers. I can do pretty awesome things."

Gianna's eyes widened. "Really?" She also whispered but didn't know why since no one else was around. "I can too! What can you do?"

"Well, after I woke up, I was trying to find a way out of these bushes, or whatever, and I turned a corner, and these three dragon-snake things came at me all at once—"

"What, three?" Gianna absently grabbed her blade, thinking of the black creature she'd put down earlier. "I had a run-in with just one of those nasty things, which was one too many. What happened?"

"I didn't have time to scream or run or nothin'. I put my hands up in front of me, and my whole body turned warm and, like, vibrated. And I hear these horrible screeching sounds, so I open my eyes and look. There's this glowing light all around me." She makes a big circle with her arms to illustrate. "And the Screechers...that's what I decided to call them, because of that sound they make...are lying on the ground, squirming like worms! I guess they ran into my force field, which I think is what I put out in front of me, and they ran into it and fell back. Then they rolled over, hissed, and shook their wings, then came at me again. So, I put my hands up again." Lucy demonstrated how she did it. "And I screamed, 'No!' Then I felt this power come out of my arms and hands, and all three screechers were thrown back, and just disappeared."

"Woah! A force field?" Gianna's eyes widened. "This is starting to sound like a Marvel movie!" Gianna clapped.

Just then, a large, incredibly muscular black man and a tall, thin blonde woman entered the courtyard through an opening in the hedge. The man's build and dress were like a professional wrestler: bare from the waist up, and from the waist down; thick belt, black spandex pants with orange flames, and black army boots. He was also bald, sporting a thin, neat goatee.

Meanwhile, the woman was like a Greek goddess in a white, flowing, spaghetti-strapped dress. She also wore a stunning, thick gold choker and white sandals laced up to the knee. Her long, golden tresses were braided and tied up on her head.

The pair hadn't yet noticed Gianna and Lucy. As they stepped toward the fountain, two more figures emerged from an opening to the left. The first was a raven-haired, bearded warrior, carrying a sword and shield. He was also bare from the waist up, except for a scarlet cloak, and leather and metal guards covered his forearms, shins, and knees.

His companion was a wild-haired old man with a grey beard, robe, and a wooden staff. As these four strangers walked toward the girls at the fountain, Gianna was extremely curious about these newcomers. Were they also from the "real world?" Were they ordinary people who now had superpowers too?

All six strangers circled the fountain, looking at each other.

Just when Gianna was about to break the awkward silence, the older gentleman spoke.

"We must all drink deeply from the fountain. Drink until you can hold no more. Then, gather at the circle of fruit trees, and I will tell you what we are to do next."

Gianna didn't question the old man's words; she just obeyed and drank, as did the others. The mist alone was invigorating and sweet, but as she began to drink the cold water, her mind seemed clearer, and the peace that she felt upon entering the courtyard and standing in the mist intensified.

For Gianna, it felt like it had been months since she had experienced any good emotions. Lately, she walked in sadness and pain; her broken heart lay open and on display, causing dark-eyed circles and possibly a permanent frown. It was only in sleep that she was able to find some peace. In fact, waking up in this place was the first time in weeks, she didn't wake up weeping. Maybe she had been brought here to find healing.

She briefly gazed at the other five strangers, all silently drinking and wondered who they were. Did they also have some secret pain? Or were they just random individuals thrown together for some cosmic game?

She looked at the old man; he had kind, wise eyes. She hoped he would have some real answers for them. It did seem strategic in some way, now that she saw there was more here like her. No, this wasn't random. Deep in her core, Gianna knew the Power that had brought them together (assuming it wasn't a dream), had a plan and purpose for this odd situation.

She continued to drink, feeling strangely composed and willing to wait the time to find the answers.

CHAPTER 2

When Diego awoke in this strange realm, he groaned as the bright sun assaulted his eyes. He rubbed them, squinting a bit until they adjusted. He slowly sat up and ran his hands through his thick mess of gray hair as he pondered the unfamiliar surroundings. He was in a beautiful garden of trees with delightful, sweet fragrances he'd never experienced before.

Immediately, the familiar, quiet inner voice of Holy Spirit began to speak to him about his assignment. Diego stood up, crossed his arms, and began to walk. The fog of sleep slowly dissipated, and dozens of questions ran through his analytical mind. His years of walking with the Lord and studying the discipline of quiet waiting had taught him to tune into communion with the Spirit easily.

Holy Spirit assured him that he was not dreaming and that he had actually entered another realm. As the physical Presence came thickly on him, he yielded to the stream of images that dropped into his spirit. Diego was excited and humbled at being chosen for this adventure. He'd never been taken to another realm to guide and pray for people before, but he figured it wasn't that different from giving a word of encouragement to a stranger on the street. He also decided it may make a good story to tell his students. "If they believe me," he chuckled out loud to himself.

He felt the Spirit join in, which made him laugh louder. The Lord proceeded to give Diego visions of a group of young people He wanted Diego to lead on a quest. As he walked, Diego was also acutely aware that he no longer had pain in his legs.

He had been shrugging off what he thought was arthritis for months, but the pain in his legs had steadily intensified. He had finally agreed to go to his physician. After many harrowing tests, Diego and his wife sat down to hear from the grim-faced doctor that he had an advanced stage of cancer. The recommended specialist was even less hopeful for a positive outcome. His wife, Nita, who had been so strong during the weeks of testing and medical visits, could no longer contain her fear and grief. She wept bitterly every day, and he was unable to comfort her.

His three beautiful, grown, and successful children still frequently came to him for advice and help. They always knew that Papa would be there for prayer, wisdom, and support, but the news of cancer changed all that.

Diego, the rock, was crumbling. He was dying, and he

struggled every day with the reality that he would have to leave his family. His usual hopeful and positive outlook had swiftly changed with the dire news. The negative prognosis and the pain were taking their toll, and he had become withdrawn, opting to take pain pills and stay in bed most days. Waking in this realm with purpose and without pain seemed to be just what he needed to lift the gray cloud. He smiled to himself with hope rising in his heart. Maybe this quest would result in a full healing.

Diego looked at the five individuals seated before him: young, unique, strong, and confused. Why he was chosen to be the Seer to lead this team on such a bizarre journey, he may never fully comprehend.

Father, why me? Why would You think these young ones would even listen to a crazy old man who says he's heard from You?

Trust Me, son. Tell them.

Yes, Father.

"You all have been called here for a purpose," Diego began. "We went to sleep last night in our beds and woke up in this world. But this is not a dream, young ones. You are awake, and this place is as real as you are."

The fragrance of the fruit trees rolled in on a soft breeze. Diego inhaled it, closed his eyes, and felt his nervous heartbeat slow down. They sat on boulders arranged in a semicircle, with Diego's rock being the largest. The grove of trees surrounding them held fruit that, with a quick glance, seemed unfamiliar, but fascinating. Rather than holding just one kind, each tree grew a variety of fruit of varying sizes, shapes, and colors.

"I woke up here just like you," Diego related, "and felt disoriented and confused at first. But as I walked, Father God began to speak to my heart. He showed me visions of each of you, and what you are to do here. Yesterday, I was a simple literature professor and family man. Today, I am the Seer sent to guide you on a journey and help you complete the task assigned to you."

"How do you know all this?" the large black man interrupted. "And how do we know you didn't bring us here, old man? How did we get here? Who do you work for? Why should we trust you?"

Some of the others nodded in agreement.

"Point taken, Darrel," Diego answered.

Darrel's eyes widened. "What? How do you know my name?"

Diego ignored the question.

"You all, understandably, have many questions. Please, allow me to finish, and I believe some of your concerns may be addressed."

Darrel still looked annoyed but didn't interrupt as Diego continued.

"God, the Creator of the Universe, brought each of us here because we are dealing with something in our lives that is hindering, binding, or enslaving us. We must overcome these obstacles, and we will not leave here until we have prevailed. Father has shown me that a great darkness is coming to our world. Each one of us will play a role in the salvation of many." He paused for emphasis. "We have also been given abilities which you should have discovered by now," He raised his staff above his head, and the top glowed brightly.

"Woah! Cool!" Lucy's eyes were wide.

He struck the ground with the bottom of the staff, the light went out, and a quick, strong wind blew over them. They squealed and put their hands over their faces.

"Another part of our task is to further develop and use these powers by fighting and defeating enemies we will encounter."

They all nodded. Gianna and Lucy looked at each other, eyes wide. Lucy then shot her hand up as if she were in class.

He smiled at her, "Yes, Ms. Lucy?"

"So, um, I have a question. If we die here, do we die for real? Or is it, like, we just wake up in our beds?"

"I'm glad you asked that great question, Lucy. The truth is, I wasn't given that information."

"Wait! What?" interjected Darrel. "That's important info, man!"

Gianna rolled her eyes. Darrel's expressive interruptions were beginning to wear on her. More to the air than to him, she said, "Look! I'm sure we weren't brought here to die." She gestured towards Diego. "Let's let him finish explaining what he knows before we overreact."

Gianna felt Darrel's stink-eye settle on her, but, in expert aloofness, she kept her eyes on the old guy.

Diego, seemingly unruffled, continued, "I absolutely understand your concern, Darrel. I was told that we would have a measure of protection here, but I want to emphasize again that this is not a dream. We are in a different realm. Different, but real—you are physically here! I can only assume that means we can get hurt and, yes, possibly even die."

Shock and fear erupted into wide eyes, and some began to stand up.

"Please! Please! Sit back down!"

"Excuse me, sir," said the bearded warrior. "Sorry to interrupt, but do we even have a choice here? Not that I don't dig this sword and powers, because they're totally cool. But I really feel like this is a super dangerous job or thing that we're heading into here, and I just feel like I need to think this through."

"Please allow me to continue, and I can give you some perspective. I do have some answers," said Diego softly.

The warrior sat back down, as did the others, hoping for more assurance than they felt at this point.

"Look, the Lord has shown me that each of us has a role to play in the salvation of our world. That just leads me to believe He wouldn't allow us to die here if we have not fulfilled our future destinies." Diego addressed the warrior and shook his head, "Lincoln, I'm sorry, but there is no choice for you here, you will have to complete this journey to go back."

He paused and looked at each person, intently.

"This is not just about you, young ones! This is about our world, your families, and friends, as well as many others! The fate of the WORLD hinges on our success!" He cracked his staff on the rock for emphasis, causing a huge boom. The team caught their breath and covered their heads, startled.

He realized his harshness and softened his voice, "Young ones, I believe it will make more sense to you as we embark on this journey, and even more will be revealed along the way."

Gianna, feeling strongly impressed to speak, stood up, "Hey, everyone, I know this sounds crazy . . . and scary, but it's not as if we haven't been given some advantages, right? We have powers, and we're doing this together?"

Lucy and Lincoln nodded.

"I mean, I have people I love back home, and if I can do something to help and protect them, I want to! And I'm hoping and praying this journey has got to be better than living like I have been the last few months."

Darrel was still scowling with arms crossed, but the beautiful blonde who hadn't said or reacted much earlier nodded vigorously at Gianna's words.

Gianna sat back down and made eye contact with their would-be leader, who managed to look calm and unfazed.

"Thank you, Gianna. We will begin by traveling to Mount Joy in the distance."

Diego pointed to the mountain peak covered with clouds beyond the forest in the distance ahead of them.

"The beginning of the path has been marked for us with red arrows. We may be attacked along the way; the enemy does not wish us to succeed. There will also be particular adversaries that can only be fought by certain individuals. The rest of us will be prevented from interfering, for it will be a physical manifestation of the affliction of the individual. As we travel on this journey, we must also come together as a team. If we stand united, trusting each other, praying for one another, and encouraging each other, we cannot fail."

Darrel was like a dark rock, arms crossed and head shaking, "I don't know, man. I'm not convinced that this isn't some wack mind-bending experiment. But I guess I'm going." He murmured and turned his head. "Not like I have a choice anyway."

Diego stroked his beard and winked playfully, "I appreciate you making the best of it, Darrel. I just ask that you be open to what Father has to show you on this journey."

Darrel didn't answer but stood up, waiting for what was next.

Diego addressed the group again, "Well, before we begin, I feel we should be properly introduced. My name is Diego, I'm a husband and father of three, and a professor at a small private university. I love my family, I love literature, and I love my students. Here, I am a Seer, which is similar to a prophet—for those who look confused."

Gianna felt a connection to Diego, who reminded her of her favorite high school teacher who had believed in her gift of writing and inspired her to develop that skill.

Darrel faced the others. "I'll go next, old man."

"It's Diego," he said firmly.

Darrel continued as if he didn't hear. "I'm Darrel Coleman, attorney at law, and when we all get back to the real world, don't hesitate to call me with any of your legal questions or situations."

He grinned widely, and Gianna half expected him to start passing out business cards, but he probably didn't have a place to keep them in his tight, flame-decorated pants.

Darrel was a large man, easily towering over all of them with powerful, handsome features, a great smile, and perfect teeth. He also exuded arrogance, and it made Gianna wary of him, besides the fact that he was a lawyer.

He was about to sit down when he remembered that he hadn't shared his ability. "Oh, and I can throw fire out of my hands and burn everything to a crisp. I finished off about five flying snake monsters in seconds." He grinned even wider and sat down.

The young warrior stood next. He was good-looking and muscular, with long, dark hair tied back, dark eyes, and a full beard. His arms, chest, and back sported a smattering of fierce, colorful tattoos, and yet he seemed friendly and humble.

"I'm Lincoln, and I'm a husband and father of four boys. I've been a youth pastor for a few years, and helping teens is my passion. I seem to be pretty good with this sword and shield, and I also have unusual strength. When I get a burning sensation in my arms, I'm almost sure I could pick up a car and throw it across a football field." Lincoln seemed to get more animated as he talked about his abilities, and he was still flexing his muscles as he sat back down.

After a moment, the blonde goddess stood up, whose piercing, crystal green eyes could be seen from a distance.

Gianna felt the turn of stomach and flush of the cheek that girls sometimes get when in the presence of superior beauty: a combination of jealousy and awe. As Gianna continued to look at the woman, she noticed a slight slump of the shoulder and the same haggard tiredness that Gianna saw in the mirror every day. This lady has known pain, she thought.

"My name is Billie Jean. I was a single mother of a beautiful little girl, but she was killed by a car almost a year ago. Currently, I'm an office manager for an online marketing company in the other world. Oh, and I'm fat in real life, so stop looking at me like that. This has to be a dream because I haven't ever been this thin." She giggled awkwardly and continued, "My ability is that I can change into a lion or an eagle."

And with that, the goddess melted away and transformed into a huge snow-white lioness with emerald green eyes. Everyone jumped back a little, startled by the sudden appearance of the beautiful, dangerous creature. As quiet as a house cat, she bounded onto a rock, lay down, and watched them all with big green eyes.

"Woah! That's impressive!" said Lincoln.

The rest stared at her, as little Lucy quietly stood up. She curiously and cautiously put her hand out to Billie Jean, who looked at her non-threateningly.

"Can I touch you?" Lucy asked the lion.

Billie Jean put her massive white head close to Lucy's hand and purred loudly. Lucy grinned and stroked her fur. Even though she was a teenager, she looked like a small child next to the big cat, and Gianna wondered if Lucy was even 100 pounds. She had noticed faint scar lines on Lucy's exposed arm as she was petting the lion, and wanted to protect her. Gianna immediately planned on sticking extra close to Lucy for the upcoming journey.

Lucy looked up at everyone as she continued to stroke the lion. "I might as well go next. I'm Lucy Ortiz. I'm sixteen and in high school. I don't know what I want to do when I graduate." All of a sudden, Lucy felt fear and uncertainty pop up as she thought of the future. She stopped petting Billie Jean and sighed, "I feel a little lost and scared about that at times." Lucy continued, "My power is that I can make force fields, and I can use a force power to blow away or throw an enemy or objects." She quickly looked away and continued to stroke the lion.

Figuring she was done, Gianna stood up. She looked at each stranger before her. Each of them was eerily familiar, like the feeling you get when you have déjà vu.

"Hey, everyone, I'm Gianna. I'm a wife and mother of a little boy. I have aspirations to be an author but have not finished a manuscript yet. Right now, I work as a freelance technical writer for websites. And my abilities include martial arts, particularly with these blades here, and strength and agility similar to Lincoln's. I get a burning feeling in my arms, and I think it makes me stronger." She smiled awkwardly and sat back down.

Diego the Seer stood back up, his thick, gray hair and unkempt beard making him look a bit fierce, but his big, kind eyes telling a completely different story. He cleared his throat, "I know you all may have more questions, but we must get moving." He gestured for them to get up, "Keep in mind that the Master is guiding us on this journey or pilgrimage if you will. He wants us to be successful and overcome. We must trust Him and have faith, no matter what comes our way."

CHAPTER 3

The party set out. They followed a path marked by red-painted arrows, first, through the fruit tree grove and then beyond into a dense forest ahead.

Diego called, "Grab some fruit and eat, if you like; I don't know when our next meal will be."

Gianna grabbed a bright pink, baseball-sized fruit from the tree closest to her. It smelled sweet and had the same texture as a plum. She bit into the soft flesh and juice dripped into her mouth and down her chin. She had no comparison for the taste, but it was the best fruit she'd ever eaten, and she consumed it greedily. When she threw the pit down, she would have gladly had another, but they were already out of the fragrant grove. Gianna noted with curiosity that she was oddly satisfied and no longer hungry, even though she calculated, it must have been a good fifteen or sixteen hours since her last meal.

As soon as the six of them passed the grove and entered the dark forest, the atmosphere changed drastically. The forest's enormous tree canopy blocked most sunlight, creating a shadowy darkness that made them shiver. Gianna looked up in awe, straining to see where the trees above her topped out. She ran her hand along the rough bark, stopped at a tree close to her, then wrapped her arms around it to see how far she could reach. Her arms didn't even span a corner of it.

"I wonder how old these trees are?" she said out loud to no one in particular.

Suddenly, a dark figure glided between the trees a few yards ahead of her. She blinked and sucked in her breath, nervously.

"I must be spooked because of the darkness," she thought, moving quickly ahead, eager to rejoin the group.

"Gianna-a-a-a…"An eerie whisper came from behind her, and the hairs on the back of her neck stood up. She quickened her stride, not daring to look back at what might have produced the creepy voice. Gianna ran the last few steps to overtake Lincoln, who brought up the rear of the party.

"Hello!" he said, a bit startled. "I didn't know you were back there. Gianna, you shouldn't stray from the group like that, this place seems dangerous on many levels."

"Oh, you noticed!" She rolled her eyes, her heart still pounding.

"What's up? Did you see something back there? He looked at the path behind her for anything suspicious.

"Well, let's just say there is something sinister in this forest, and it knows my name."

"What do you mean?" Lincoln raised his eyebrows.

"Um...if I'm not losing my mind, I think I saw a dark figure floating between the trees." She pointed back to the area she had come from. "And when I turned to get the heck outta' there, it whispered my name. So, I'm pretty freaked out right now." Gianna's explanation made her more nervous than she was before, and she crossed her arms.

Lincoln nudged Gianna in front of him, "I'll take the rear for a while. Let's try to catch up with the others and stick close together. If nothing else, at least being close may make us feel better.

She nodded and walked ahead, grateful not to be alone on such a journey.

Up ahead, Darrel looked around nervously, his heart thumping loudly. He took a few deep breaths, attempting to calm himself. Darrel knew his mind was messing with him, and it was unnerving that a little darkness could shake him up so much. He was never fond of darkness or nature, and the combination made for a grumpy boy. He thought he kept hearing low whispers from the trees, saying, "Diiiiiie, Diiiie...Daaarel...Diiiie." The old man and little girl were walking a bit in front of him. Billie Jean, in lion form, strode ahead of the whole group. The further they walked, the more on edge Darrel became. He kept clenching and unclenching his hands, which caused static electricity to move through his arms and down to his fingers. The whispers seemed to be getting more frequent and coming from different directions.

Darrel's increasing fear and anxiety were making him breathless and jumpy. As his heart hammered in his ears, sweat streamed down his head and back. He decided to stop walking to hear more clearly and willed his heart to slow down. Immediately, there was an abrupt silence. Suddenly, something cold and leathery brushed by Darrel's left ear.

"Diiiiiie!"

He jumped with a shout of terror and shot flames, igniting a tree nearby. Lucy screamed—startled by the sudden flame. Darrel, still frantic and jumpy, had his arms set and ready to attack again. He saw no movement but heard evil snickering all around. The others gathered around him, and Diego asked if something had attacked him.

"You don't hear the voices?!" His eyes wild with fright, "They're everywhere! Creepy voices, whispering my name!"

The old man looked at him, thoughtfully stroking his beard. Gianna and Lincoln caught up.

"Hey, is everyone okay? What's all the commotion about?" asked Lincoln with sword drawn and ready.

Darrel had his hands on his hips, "There is some crazy, evil stuff in the dark woods, man. I'm about to burn this whole place down."

"I heard something back there too—from the trees," added Gianna.

Darrel nodded vigorously and pointed at Gianna, "See! She heard it too. I'm not crazy, y'all!"

Lucy looked puzzled. She hadn't heard or seen anything. As Billie Jean transformed back into "Amazing Goddess," she shook her head, "I didn't either." She looked at Darrel apologetically, "Sorry, Darrel."

Diego asked Gianna and Darrel what the voices had said.

"I only heard one whisper, and it said my name, and it

was creepy, creepy, creepy," Gianna answered, rubbing her arms nervously.

Darrel nodded again. "Same here, whispery voices kept telling me to die, and then something touched my head. I still hear them, by the way." He shivered.

Diego shushed them and stepped away, closing his eyes. A minute or so later, he walked back. "Yes, I feel the evil from the forest—but I do not hear or see anything. It seems to be picking out certain individuals to manifest to, maybe to divide and conquer."

He went to Darrel and Gianna, placing his hand on Darrel's arm. Darrel seemed to visibly relax, "Darrel, Gianna, all of you." Lucy and Lincoln got closer, Billie Jean placed her hand on Darrel's. Diego continued, "No matter what you feel, see or hear, you must believe and understand that the power in you is greater than the power in this world. This evil is limited, and just like in our world, it relies on fear and deception to defeat you. We will get through this forest together in faith."

With that, he walked ahead of them. Billie Jean squeezed Darrel's hand and let go. Before he could respond, she turned back into a lioness and bounded along behind Diego. Lucy and Lincoln followed. Gianna and

Darrel continued at the back of the line, making sure to stay close to the others.

After a bit of time, Diego felt the darkness come over him like a blanket. Instinctively, he began to recite the verses of Psalm 23 quietly to himself as they walked. "Even though I walk through the valley of the shadow of death, I will fear no evil, for thou art with me. . ."

As a child who suffered night terrors, Diego quickly learned that he needed peace from God to overcome the paralyzing fear that overcame him nightly. His mother helped him memorize the psalm that soon became an anchor to him. For the rest of his life, in times of fear, and even daily, the 23rd Psalm helped Diego remember that his Good Shepherd was always with him. Meanwhile, as he recited, he kept his eyes sharply fixed on the path ahead, while tuning his spirit senses to the danger closing around them.

Suddenly, Diego caught sight of a large, dark, moving figure far beyond the trees and steadied his senses for what was coming. The figure seemed to be following them as they walked, slinking from tree to tree. Then, to the left, he saw another one.

Diego continued to whisper the psalm, "I will not fear,

for thou art with me. . .” He heard snickering from the darkness.

Lucy edged closer to him and grabbed his hand, “Professor, did you hear that?”

“Yes, hija. Don’t worry; God is with us.” He looked over at her and squeezed her hand. “Why did you call me ‘professor’?”

She giggled nervously. “I don’t know, really. You said you were a teacher, and it seemed better than ‘mister’ or ‘old man’.”

“I like it. My students call me ‘professor’ at school. Stay close to me, hija.”

“What does Hija mean?” Lincoln had come up behind the Seer and the teen.

“Daughter,” answered Lucy, and smiled.

Lincoln pulled his sword, “Is it just me, Professor, or does it feel . . .” He paused, grasping for words, “... charged? Like when someone is staring you down, and you know you’re about to fight them?”

Lucy let go of Diego’s hand and engaged her force field like a shield on her body.

Diego nodded. “Yes, Lincoln. Even though we can’t

see anything, the spiritual atmosphere is most definitely charged with dark energy aimed at us."

Within minutes, a horrifying scream came from deep in the forest. The six travelers gathered close in various fighting stances back to back.

Get Ready.

The still small voice spoke to Diego.

"Get ready!" Diego spoke aloud to the others.

Suddenly, it sounded like a great rush of bat squeals and wings were descending on them. Lucy stood in the center of the group with her arms lifted up, enfolding them all in a force field. A multitudinous mass of black creatures swirled around them, and then landed just in front of Diego, directly blocking their path.

It was a great throng of writhing teeth, wings, and squeaks until the figures slowly solidified into one massive, dark shape. Surrounded by a grey mist, it stood over ten feet tall, clad from head to toe in thick, black metal armor, and a broad and tall helmet, with five large points protruding from the top. The eyes peering out of the helmet were like yellow flame, and in its great metal fist, it held a gnarly, spiked mace.

For a moment, no one moved. Then Lincoln said quietly to the group, "We are going to die! That's the Witch King from Lord of the Rings!"

The adversary stepped forward. The six heroes immediately screamed and grabbed their heads as ghastly images filled their minds: bloody corpses, suffering souls in hell, war, torture, and many more horrors than a human mind could handle before cracking with madness.

Lucy's force field faltered, then broke. One by one, they began to fall to the ground, squirming from the hellish images. Only Diego still stood facing the enemy as he managed to sputter, "No…weapon...formed against...me will...prosper! Greater is He...that is within me... than he that is within the world!" Then the Seer struck the end of his staff on the ground and shouted, "Stop, fiend! You will come no closer in the mighty name of Jesus Christ!"

An unholy scream rang out from behind the dark enemy, and he faltered. The grotesque images suddenly stopped, and the group slowly began to stand up again. The enemy raised his mace, and the thick mist parted, revealing an army of dark, nightmarish figures behind him. Only the front few were clearly visible to Diego and the group. Each creature was disgustingly different. Many were some form of animal-monster—resembling boars, bats, and gorillas, many with wings and talons, most sported fangs and horns, which protruded from faces and bodies.

The Dark Leader lowered his weapon and spoke, but the words came from the surrounding forest instead of any visible mouth.

"Today, you will die in this place, and we will feast on your flesh." Agreeing grunts, howls, and cackles sounded from the ugly mob behind him.

Darrel whispered to Lincoln, "I keep pinchin' myself, but I can't seem to wake up from this nightmare."

Lincoln nodded in agreement, "I think I just soiled my britches; I hope that doesn't slow me down."

Gianna and Diego both prayed silently. Billie Jean, still in lion form crouched down, ears flattened, fangs out, with a deep rumbling coming from her belly. Lucy kept close to Diego, unsuccessfully trying to lift her force field over the group again.

Meanwhile, Diego felt a secure peace and courage come over him. The enemy had faltered at his command a moment ago. He stood tall with his staff still stuck firmly in the ground in front of him. He felt assured that God would come through. They had a mission to accomplish.

Diego, I am with you. Do you trust Me? The Spirit's question appeared strongly in his mind.

Diego was unwavering in his response. *Yes, Lord.*

Diego, do you trust Me? He asked again.

Yes, Lord, of course, I do. He wondered why Father had asked him a second time.

Child, do you believe I will take care of the others if you fall?

He was nonplussed. *Yes, Lord.*

Diego, do you believe I will take care of your family if you die?

Diego was startled by the last question. *M-My Father... of course You will. Why are you asking me this now?*

Step forward, My son.

Diego raised his staff and obediently stepped toward the evil horde. As he moved, a piercing white light appeared around them, and another intense, hair-raising scream erupted from the dark army. Diego shielded his eyes from the light while attempting to see where it was coming from. He got a brief glimpse of a mass of white-winged warriors encircling them. The nasty, evil army advanced on the angels in full force, but not a blow landed. The speed at which the heavenly warriors moved was almost too fast for Diego and the others to fully see. But soon, the dark creatures began to slow their press as they realized it was a futile endeavor. Many began to turn and run.

Diego's team laughed and cheered as they witnessed the impressive spectacle. The dark leader seemed to have already disappeared, but his voice projected loudly from the forest, above the screams of his army.

"It's not over! We will return and destroy the six chosen vessels!"

Suddenly, the screaming ceased, and the remaining enemy horde faded back into the darkness of the forest. The great white light began to fade, and on the path in front of the travelers stood one of the angelic warriors, dressed in golden armor with a sword in hand.

He was altogether majestic, holy, and fearsome. The glory light, though faded, was still visible around his eight-foot muscular frame. "Greetings, mighty warriors of El Elyon!" They looked at each other, wondering who he was talking to.

Diego bowed, and the others followed his example.

"Please rise," said the angel. "I too serve the Almighty, He alone is worthy of reverence."

They all stood up at his words.

"I am here to encourage you. The Most High has sent us to go with you on this journey, though you won't be able to see us. We will not intervene in all the trials but will be here when you need us most. Beware, the enemy seeks to defeat you and try many different ways to turn you from your path. You will be strengthened and equipped as each of you defeats your personal adversary."

All of a sudden, the whole troop of angel warriors encircled the group and spread their immense, shining wings. They began to slowly wave their wings, causing a soft breeze with a sweet fragrance to fall on the group. Gianna closed her eyes as she inhaled the heavenly scent. Pictures began to flood her mind: a sunrise over an ocean, mountain peaks covered with snow, the first time she saw her newborn son.

Each new image was like a balm to their minds, causing some outbursts of tears and laughter. Gianna began to understand that these images were replacing and canceling out the previous horrible ones they experienced from the enemy.

After a few minutes, the fragrance and images faded. Each of them began to come out of the experience and stand to their feet. The angels were gone, and the forest was once again dark and sinister. Their smiles of joy changed quickly to frowns of disappointment. Diego motioned for them to gather close. He put his arm around Lucy and faced the others, "Don't be afraid, young ones. The heavenly host is still with us. Let's move on, though." "The sooner we move on, the sooner we get free of this terrible place." The group nodded to him, and a few extra hugs went around before they followed Diego's lead forward.

CHAPTER 4

It seemed like they had been walking for hours through the forest, following the red arrows as they appeared on random trees along the path. Whether it was night or day, they couldn't tell, as light could not penetrate the dense forest canopy. It felt like the further they walked, the darker it became. Darrel kept a fireball blazing in his hand, while the others had made a couple of torches to bring them some small comfort.

They walked, sometimes in pairs, sometimes singly, depending on the size of the path. Diego usually led with Lucy beside or close behind him. Billie Jean walked next to Darrel, occasionally in human form. But when in lion form, she would move to the head of the team. Gianna and Lincoln were typically last, walking with blades drawn.

There was a bit of talking among them, but more often silence, for it seemed the darkness was thick with sinister sounds that often drowned out their conversations. Other times, it was completely quiet, and they could hear their own hearts beat as they trekked. During these soundless phases, the silence became more frightening than the loud squawks, squeals, and snickers that they frequently heard.

It was like something was waiting to jump out and attack at any moment.

"What images did you see in your mind when the angels were with us?" Lincoln asked Gianna, breaking a particularly long silence.

She smiled as she remembered. "Well, one was when my son was born, and the doctor first put him in my arms. We looked at each other, then I kissed his tiny perfect hand, and for the first time in my life, God was real." She smiled to herself at the vivid memory. "I couldn't stop crying; I felt God in the room with me. That was when I gave Him my whole heart and knew that I would be His forever."

"That's beautiful," he said. "I have boys too. Four amazing, handsome, and unique sons."

"Wow! Four?" Her eyes widened, then she smiled. "Aren't boys awesome?"

"Yeah," he chuckled and sighed as he thought about each boy and how much he wanted to be a good father to them.

"How old are they?"

"10, 7, and 2-year-old twins."

"Oh, my goodness! I bet there is a lot of energy and noise at your house!" said Gianna.

"Oh yeah! Our wrestling matches get pretty wild!" Lincoln laughed. "My wife, Charlotte, used to try to break it up, but she learned after the first two that it's best to let us go at it and burn up all that energy."

Gianna giggled, thinking of her husband and son having their own loud and crazy play matches. It was nice to remember the good times for a change.

Talking about their children seemed to lighten the mood for a time, but slowly the darkness crept back in, melting away the positive feelings they had conjured up with their memories; they grew quiet again. Both Gianna and Lincoln began walking like they were on autopilot, barely registering steps and time, as they became entrenched in deep thought of pains that plagued their souls.

Lincoln's pace had slowed to the point that he had fallen behind the whole group. His thoughts wandered to his recent moral failures. Shame about his pornography addiction, at times, felt like a lead weight around his neck. His emotions churned as his love for his family compelled him with a deep desire to fight and overcome the shackles— ones he knew could destroy what he loved the most. His wife and boys' faces surfaced in his thoughts. Had he just put the boys to bed last night? He remembered hugging and kissing his twins, James and Jacob before thumbs popped in mouths and teddies were snuggled close. The oldest, Chris, who felt he was too old for kisses, laid down with a quick hug and smile. Then there was Petey, still young enough to bear hug and cling close, finally laying down next to Lincoln's sweet, beautiful wife, Charlie.

She drifted to sleep, snuggled up against Petey, and tears had filled Lincoln's eyes as he was reminded of how he'd hurt her. His addiction had consumed him for years, but in the past few months, he had been worse than ever. His inability to control it was now affecting every aspect of his life.

Most recently, the loss of his youth pastoring job almost completely destroyed his reputation. Thankfully, he had submitted his resignation before he got fired. But the embarrassment to his wife and her hurt and pain were almost too much for him to bear. He felt distance between them growing every day, and he felt powerless to stop it. His years of prayers, he believed, had fallen on deaf ears. The shame kept him from asking for help from church leaders who were often judgmental. Where could he go?

He was on the edge of a precipice: about to fall off or fling himself from it. And just as he was thinking about leaving his family, he woke up in this place.

Lincoln glanced ahead, pulling himself from his thoughts, and noticed that Gianna and Lucy were yards away from him; he could barely make them out as they walked amid dense trees. He wiped away a stray tear from his cheek and began to quicken his pace to catch up.

All of a sudden, to his left, he heard faint music. He stopped, gripped his sword hilt at his side, and slowed his breathing to listen. In the distance, he heard a faint song, and while he couldn't make out the words, the melody seemed familiar. He was so intrigued that he felt compelled to take a closer look. He walked off the path, picking and prodding his way through the branches toward the source of the music. As he got closer, he heard what he thought was a flowing stream nearby.

Lincoln peered through a break in the trees and saw a waterfall flowing into a small pool. Standing in the pool was a naked woman bathing and singing. Behind her, in the distance, was a luxurious sprawling field with undulating green and wildflower-speckled hills.

The woman was immersed in the water up to her waist,

her long fiery red hair fell down her back in ringlets. Her skin was porcelain white, and her body: voluptuous perfection. Lincoln's heart beat faster, and his breath quickened as he watched her bathe. He didn't dare move for fear of startling her, but he strained for a closer look.

Gianna and Lucy caught up to Darrel.

"Can you see where we're heading?" Gianna asked him.

Darrel grunted, gesturing to their surroundings, "I see what you see. Trees. This place is a mind trip."

Gianna rolled her eyes at his snarky answer.

Lucy looked behind them, "Hey, where's Lincoln?"

"He probably just fell behind a little bit. Maybe he's sightseeing. I'll go check."

Darrel ran back down the path and yelled Lincoln's name. There was no response.

A few minutes later, he ran back, "No sign of him. We better go tell the Professor and Catwoman to hold up."

Diego and Billie Jean had already stopped when they saw the others weren't with them.

"Professor! Billie Jean!" Lucy called out. "We gotta' go

back; Lincoln's gone!"

Diego said something to Billie Jean. The lioness bounded back toward them, transformed into a snow-white eagle, and flew back towards where they had last seen Lincoln.

Gianna ran back down the path after her, and the others followed close behind. She began to feel the familiar tingling in her legs and noticed the trees start to blur beside her as she sped past them. The sound of a waterfall, sudden and out of place, caused her to slow down to investigate.

As Lincoln watched the lady in the pool, he felt powerless to turn away, even though he knew that he should. He strained to see more, yet still, stay concealed so as not to scare the woman. The urgent thought that he should turn and run was suddenly interrupted as he spied a giant snake slip into the pool and swim towards the lady. Lincoln threw his shield down, grabbed his dagger, and ran into the water.

The woman stopped singing and watched as he crashed through the underbrush and jumped into the pool. He quickly grabbed the snake, which was bigger and stronger than he thought. He held it behind its neck, barely keeping its open jaw from his face. Holding his dagger, Lincoln stabbed it through the bottom of its jaw into its head. The reptile stopped fighting and went limp as Lincoln threw the snake's body onto the bank.

Breathing heavily, he turned back toward the beautiful woman. From far away, she was stunning, but up close, she was beyond words. Her sky-blue eyes sparkled in the sunlight, making his stomach flutter, and he flushed like a schoolboy.

"Thank you, kind sir," her voice captured him.

She smiled as Lincoln consumed her with his eyes. He noticed that she didn't try to cover her nakedness, and he finally looked away shyly.

Gianna moved closer to the water noise she had heard earlier and continued to make her way toward the sound. Soon she came through the brush to a clearing, where she observed Lincoln being led by a naked woman, out of a pool, and onto a grassy bank. The lady was singing to him as he followed her toward the hills. His eyes were locked on her as she coaxed him like a teacher with a child.

Gianna's stomach dropped, and she began to panic.

Somehow this scene was triggering her. A feeling of déjà vu came over her, and she shivered. She had to get Lincoln out of here. She tried to run through the break in the trees, but they were like an iron barricade. The harder she tried, it seemed the denser and more unyielding the trees got. She then began to yell to Lincoln, but it was as if he was in a soundproof room; he and the woman never even turned towards her.

Gianna heard an eagle squawk and saw Billie Jean circling above the couple. The white eagle began to dive, aiming towards the woman but then bounced back as if she hit a rubber wall. Billie Jean landed in the trees below and shook her head and feathers out, stunned.

Lincoln and the woman were getting further away every second. Worried, Gianna ran back to find the others. Meanwhile, she was wondering why the woman seemed so familiar. Just as she got back to the path, she stopped and snapped her fingers.

That was it! I remember her!

Just then, the others caught up. Gianna grabbed Diego's arm. "Professor, Lincoln is being led away by a woman and Billie Jean, and I can't get through to him. He can't hear us!"

Billie Jean landed and changed into her human form. "I flew down on them and was knocked back by some invisible barrier. I wonder if any of us can get through."

"It's quite possible that Lincoln is in the throes of his enemy. We may not be able to intervene in this trial," Diego answered.

"I bet I can get through!" Darrell's arms and hands flamed up, and he stalked towards the waterfall.

The others followed behind him. Gianna walked with Diego, "Professor, another thing that is worrying me is that this woman looks like a character out of a story I've read."

The Seer paused. "Really? What story?"

Gianna took Diego's hand and pulled him forward, "You have to see her; I'm almost certain it's her: La Belle Dame sans Merci."

Diego's eyes widened, "La Belle Dame! Could it be?"

They reached the tree clearing as Darrel tried to muscle his way through. He stopped and grunted as sweat poured down his face. "Everyone, back up! I'm gonna' barbeque these trees!"

They moved, and flames flowed out of Darrel's hands, but nothing happened to the trees—not even a single singed leaf. Darrel's eyes were round with disbelief. "What the h-"

"Okay, Darrel," Gianna hurriedly moved around him. "Let Diego and me through; we need him to see if the woman is La Belle Dame sans Merci."

"La belle, who?" Darrel scrunched his face at her.

Diego ran to the opening and watched as the red-haired siren led Lincoln further away from them. He caught his breath, "Hay Dios Mio! Can it be?"

"It is her, isn't it, Professor?" Gianna's feelings of concern mounted by the minute.

He nodded toward Darrel and stroked his beard thoughtfully. "La Belle Dame sans Merci is a ballad written by John Keats. The title is French, and in English, it means 'The Beautiful Lady without Pity.'"

"Hey!" exclaimed Lucy. "I think I read that in my English Lit class at school! It's about a knight getting bewitched by a fairy lady."

Gianna nodded, "Yes, the knight meets a beautiful lady in a field and gets entranced by her. Doesn't he get trapped on the hill in a depression, Professor, like always sighing and weeping?"

"Some think that it is simply a fairy story and no more, while others feel it is full of moral symbolism." Diego leaned on his staff and continued, "The knight and the lady are symbolic of breaking a vow and lust. The knight is forever doomed to remain on the hillside as a result of this sin. The lady can also represent a demonic entrapment to sexual sin, and the unwary knight a victim."

The others stood silent, feeling helpless as they pondered Diego's words. Gianna readily gripped her blades as she tried to quickly think of how to use this new information to help Lincoln.

Meanwhile, Darrel shook his head and laughed nervously. "So, you're tryin' to tell me that Lincoln is trapped in a story with some devil woman?"

The Seer nodded, "Yes, that may be the case."

"So, how do we help him then?" Darrel growled with frustration. "None of us can get through."

"Darrel, this is Lincoln's challenge," Diego gently explained. "What we can do is pray and intercede for him to be strong and overcome the power of the Evil One."

"Man, that's like doing nothin'!" Darrel barked back with anger and concern. "Why won't God let us help him?!"

"Don't underestimate the power of prayer, my friend." Diego placed his hand on Darrel's arm and looked him in the eye. "The great prophet Elijah prayed that it wouldn't rain, and it didn't rain in Israel for three years! Joshua of old prayed for the sun and moon to stand still until Israel defeated the Amorites in battle, and the sun didn't move for a full day!" Diego pointed at Lincoln and the lady. "What can your prayers do?"

Lincoln's eyes were locked on the Lady, and he was powerless to look away. His stomach was in knots, for he knew he should run from her, yet he also yearned for her and couldn't stop drinking her body in with his eyes. He was partially aware that something wasn't quite right, and the pangs of danger ringing in his gut seemed like a car alarm, noticeable, yet also blending into the background noise. Her voice, her movements, and her body drew him both to the edges of desire and madness with every step, causing the pinging warnings to drown in the deep bodily yearnings he had never experienced until this day.

Some faint whisper of warning still scratched at the corner of his consciousness which caused him to wonder, what in the actual hell he was doing. The Beauty led him further and further away, frequently touching his face or arm and singing another rapturous melody, and the fleeting thought of fear would leave. As he looked at her lips, his mouth watered like a starving dog; to kiss her mouth would be heavenly, to touch her body would be euphoric. His body seemed to move of its own will as his mind and heart continued to fight weakly against the onslaught.

Lincoln, pray.

He turned his eyes from the Lady and put his hand to his chest, as if in pain, and answered The Still Small Voice he knew so well.

My Master, help me, please. His heart cried out.

Softly and clearly, the voice answered, *I'm right here, Lincoln. I've never left.*

I don't want to do this, Lord...but I'm so weak.

My strength is made perfect in your weakness, my son.

Lincoln's eyes filled up, and he fell to his knees on the grass. The Enchantress stroked his face and beard, as she gazed deeply into his eyes, still singing softly. The touch of her hand to his face, her exquisite body inches from his, and the alluring sound of her voice drew him to his feet. She held tight to his hand and led him further yet into the green hills, further away from the woods and the others. His heart ached in him, tears trailed down his cheeks, yet his feet kept moving forward. Then a voice cried out his name, "Lincoln!"

He stopped and looked back; his sweet Charlie's voice came to him across the field. "Charlie?"

He saw her face in his mind and the pain in her eyes as if she were fully aware of his betrayal of her; it was all he could do not to cry out.

"He heard me, Professor!" Gianna screamed, still focused on Lincoln. She continued to jump up and down and wave her arms frantically. "Just now, when I called his name, he turned to look!"

Diego looked up at her from where he was praying. He was the only one still on his knees. The others had given up shortly after starting and instead were watching Lincoln with increasing worry and concern. Gianna had still prayed, but she also took to shouting at Lincoln, even though it seemed useless. Darrel and Lucy joined her in hollering, but he still seemed unable to hear or see them. Meanwhile, Billie Jean continued to fly circles above the

Lady and Lincoln, hoping that there would eventually be a way in for her.

The Lady tried to pull him, but he yanked back his hand and began to move away from her. She walked slowly toward him, still singing, her hair blown back by the breeze so that he could see every part of her. He began to tremble and closed his eyes to block her out. In his mind, he began to recite a Scripture, "For the weapons of our warfare are not carnal but mighty in God for pulling down strongholds and every high thing that exalts itself against the knowledge of God, bringing every thought into captivity to the obedience of Christ!"

As he finished saying these words, a hellish scream pierced the air, and he opened his eyes.

The Lady had transformed into a red reptilian creature, its gaping maw of razors spread wide. He screamed and backed up quickly, but not quick enough to avoid being slashed in the side with a long dagger-like claw. He yelled as pain flooded through his entire body. Lincoln grabbed his bloody side, turned, and ran. The waterfall and the green hills behind faded into a thick gray mist all around him.

"Help me, Lord!" he cried out.

The Waking

He felt the tingling sensation in his legs, and soon the forest was coming up fast.

Diego went to the frantic shouters and put his hands on them. "Young ones, young ones, please! Stop this shouting; it is useless! He cannot hear us. Our job is to pray. We can't get through to him, but the Lord can."

Darrel turned back to the clearing, "Look! He's running back this way!"

"He's hurt and bleeding!" Gianna felt on the edge of panic. "That monster is going to kill him!"

Darrel tried again to run through the shrubs but was still held back by the barrier. "We still can't help him?!"

As he was speaking, a blur whipped by his face, and they all gasped. Billie Jean flew above them. "That was Lincoln!" she called out as she flew after him.

Gianna looked back at the clearing, and the monster was gone as well as the pool, waterfall, and rolling hills. All that was there was brush and the inky darkness of the forest. Amazed, she put her hand through the shrub area that a moment ago was an invisible barrier.

"Come on!" shouted Lucy as she waved them on.

They all ran after Lincoln and found him a few yards ahead lying on the ground and Billie Jean kneeling over him. She was holding his cloak over the wound, trying to stop the blood. He was pale as a sheet and writhing and groaning in pain. Billie Jean looked up, her eyes watering, "It looks really bad; he's lost so much blood! What are we going to do?!"

Diego went over and knelt on the other side of him; he nodded at Billie Jean, who let go of the cloak as he uncovered the wound. Gianna sucked in her breath, "Oh no!"

There were three deep, ugly gashes across his left side, and blood was pouring out. Immediately, Diego put a hand on the wound and looked up to heaven and prayed:

"Heavenly Father, Have mercy on your servant, Lincoln, Who has fought the good fight of faith, and followed your word by fleeing from Lust, as Joseph of old did from Potipher's wife. Heal his wounds, that he may complete the task You have called us to!

Glorify Your Name in our generation, Adonai!

We come together in faith, believing that you are not through with this man, and it is not Your will for him to die in this place. I pray this in the name of the Messiah Jesus, Amen."

As they watched the man of God pray, a brilliant light came out of Diego's hand—or was it out of the wound itself? It was hard to tell, but the light shone for a moment and disappeared. As Diego continued to pray quietly over him, Lincoln's face and body visibly relaxed, and he seemed to be peacefully asleep. After some time, Diego slowly removed his hand from what had been a sizeable gaping mess of a bloody wound. They all gasped as all that was left of the damage was just a red smear of dried blood.

Lucy squealed and jumped up and down, "He's healed! It's gone!"

Gianna wiped away tears as she, Billie Jean, and Lucy shared a hug. Suddenly, Darrel picked them up in a giant bear hug, squeezing them together; they laughed hysterically.

Lincoln, having been roused by the laughter, attempted to sit up.

"Waas happening...?" he asked groggily. Diego gently had him lay back down, "Rest a bit, Lincoln, you've been through an affliction, my friend."

Lincoln nodded his head and drifted back to sleep. The group decided to stay where they were to let Lincoln rest for a bit longer. After about an hour, Diego roused

Lincoln and urged the team to get up. He reminded them that resting for too long in the forest was dangerous. Darrel grabbed Lincoln's hand and pulled him up, Lincoln groaned still feeling a bit weak, "Thanks, man!" Lincoln clapped him on the shoulder.

Darrel nodded and winked, "Hey Link, I'm glad you're okay. We were worried."

"Thanks, Darrel," Lincoln looked at him a bit surprised. "that means a lot, man."

The two men continued to walk at the tail of the group, noticing that the forest was still dark and eerily quiet. Darrel walked with one arm lit, the light helping him feel calmer in the fearsome surroundings.

Darrel spoke to Lincoln, "We saw what was happening to you and tried to get through to help, but there was some crazy force field, and we couldn't."

"Oh . . ." Lincoln looked down, a little embarrassed. "You guys saw everything?"

Darrel flashed his perfect smile and punched Lincoln on the shoulder, "Hey man, don't worry. We know you were being, like, mind-controlled by that beautiful devil-woman. Hey, I probably would've run too, ya know?"

Lincoln nodded sheepishly but didn't respond.

"Hey, man," Darrel said after a few minutes of quiet.

It took a moment for Lincoln to reply as if he was pulling away from deep thoughts. "Yeah, what's up, brother?"

"I'm curious, ya' know, after what went down earlier with the healing. What did you feel? Do you remember it?"

After a few moments of walking in silence, Darrel thought Lincoln wasn't going to answer. And then he heard him choking back a sob. "I thought I was going to die, man . . . it was so painful."

Lincoln touched his side at the memory. "It was like every part of my body was on fire. And that wasn't the worst of it...my heart was breaking with how I had failed." He shook his head and wiped a tear that had escaped. Then, it all stopped."

"Stopped?" Darrel raised his eyebrows.

"Yeah. The burning in my body and the anguish in my mind." He snapped his fingers. "Just like that."

Darrel shook his head, "That was pretty trippy, man. If I hadn't seen that gash close up with my own eyes, I wouldn't have believed it."

Lincoln looked at Darrel. "Hey man," He took a deep

breath. "I really want to thank y'all for trying to help me . . . and praying for me. Like, I know I could've died back there."

Darrel nodded and shrugged, "Well, really no need to thank me for prayin' because I didn't do much of that." He chuckled lightly, "I guess I tried doing it 'the hard way' because I kept going at an immovable force-field and the old—" He caught himself. "Diego, man, he never stopped praying. And I guess I really believe that's what made the difference."

Lincoln smiled, "I'm just thankful for all of you. Whether you prayed or not, it's so cool to know there's someone there for you." He ran his hand absently through his hair and took a breath, "Even being in this strange world, and almost dying! It's like I'm starting to understand why we're here!"

Darrel squinted his eyes at him, "Okay? So, you look like dying earlier was a good thing." He gestured to the air. "So, convince me, dude."

"Darrel, I feel like a new person! It's like I have a second chance." He paused, grinning as if a lightbulb had come on over his head. He turned to Darrel. "I went to bed in the other world without any hope that I could change and be a better man. Now, after coming through that nightmare...I believe I can, with God, actually, be a better man!"

Darrel was thoughtful about what Lincoln had said.

"Man, I don't know about all that," Darrel shook his head. "Good for you. But, I don't think almost dying is going to fix anything for me."

Lincoln stroked his beard, "Say what you will, my friend, but I have a feeling you're not getting out of this place the same as you came in."

Darrel shrugged his shoulders uncomfortably, grumbled a bit, and walked on ahead of Lincoln, abruptly ending the conversation. He moved to the front near Diego but walked on without engaging the Seer.

Gianna slowed her pace to let Lincoln catch up, and they briefly engaged in surface conversation about how he was feeling. Although she felt compelled to ask him about the deeper issues, she opted for light banter instead. Something was bothering her that she was not quite ready to address, so she kept it to herself and felt that another time for getting more personal would present itself. For now, the dark forest path compelled them to trek further into the unknown, and the travelers grew quiet, wondering about their families in the other world.

CHAPTER 5

Gianna soon became lost in thought again, which was easy with the seemingly endless walking. Lincoln's ordeal had scared her in so many ways. Foremost, it was her inability to help him as it made her wonder if they each were going to be left on their own to fight mortally dangerous battles.

For another thing, she couldn't shake Lincoln's particular struggle with the woman who seemed to embody lust and adultery. It hit uncomfortably close to home, and Gianna felt the pull of sadness and hurt in the pit of her gut. She had hoped to leave the familiar, binding feelings behind. Waking up in this strange world without the constant heavy pain had her believing that she may have been healed, but apparently, that was not the case.

Wanting to ask Diego for his thoughts, Gianna moved to catch up to him but realized she must have fallen way behind. It had been a while since she had heard the others' footsteps or conversations. She stopped and listened intently. Beginning to get nervous, she called out ahead of her, "Diego! Lincoln!"

She ran a bit ahead but still didn't find anyone. It was still dark, except for swathes of moonlight peeking through the trees above. She heard a voice and stopped abruptly. Her heart beat in her ears, and she took deep breaths to try to slow it down so she could hear better. Laughter came from the surrounding forest.

"Hello?! Lucy?!" She looked around, trying to figure out which direction the sound had come from. "Anyone?"

Again, she heard laughter, a woman's laugh, from somewhere in the dark of the forest. She didn't want to leave the path, knowing it was unwise and dangerous, but she also was curious about it, because the sound was oddly familiar to her. Soon enough, she heard it again and thought she'd just wander slightly off the path towards the sound to see if she knew the source of the voice.

"Come closer, Gianna," a woman's voice called out. "Come to me."

Then more laughter.

The hair rose at the back of her neck at the mention of her name. After some plodding through thick brush and leaves, she finally found a break in the trees leading to an open area. Scattered around the area, encircling a central platform, were flaming stone columns that cast an eerie light and shadow on surrounding objects. At first, she thought she had come upon a crowd of people surrounding the stone platform upon which a lone figure sat. After watching the crowd for a few moments and seeing no movement, she soon realized they were actually a collection of human-shaped stone statues.

Gianna inched closer to the platform with the mystery figure and examined the array of statues. Each statue was in various poses: a warrior with his sword drawn, a maiden holding a basket, a man with eyes gazing at the sky, and many others. As a literature and movie geek, Gianna couldn't help but jump to the conclusion that these were people who had been turned to stone. Since she still couldn't fully make out what the seated woman in the center looked like, Gianna's mind followed the theme and assumed the woman might be Medusa.

She tried to remember the old film she saw as a child, *Clash of the Titans*.

How did they defeat her?

All she could come up with was that they used a shield as a mirror either to see her or for her to look at herself?

Doesn't matter; I don't have a shield.

Gianna stopped close enough to see better, but still far enough away that she thought the laughing lady would have to come down from the platform and a bit further out to get to her. The woman stood up. She wore a dark cloak with the cowl shadowing her face, and Gianna quickly looked to the side, just in case it was Medusa. She definitely didn't want to be turned to stone.

"Gianna, I'm so glad you could come," the mysterious lady said, still in an amused voice. Gianna wondered what she could have been so amused by since there didn't seem to be anything here that was funny. The woman must be crazy.

Watch yourself, Gianna.

She then whispered a quick prayer, "Oh God, please protect me."

I'm sorry. Do we know each other?"

The woman replied, "I've been very involved in your life lately, Gianna. I'm so glad we are finally meeting face to face." She threw the hood back, exposing a wide Cheshire grin.

"I don't understand. What do you have to do with me?" Gianna asked, looking closely at the woman's hair: jet black, long, and glossy. No snakes.

She had a small sigh of relief at not having to deal with Medusa. She now felt safe to look directly at her.

"What's the matter, Gianna? Are you afraid to look at me?" More laughter, which revealed scary, long fangs surrounded by blood-red lips.

Gianna shivered.

Eww. She's probably worse than dealing with a cursed titan.

The woman was tall, slender, and pale, with a regal posture exuding elitist sentiment. Her eyes seemed to glow red, or it could have been a reflection of the firelight.

"Who are you?" Gianna asked challengingly.

"You may have heard of me." She answered proudly, standing erect on her stone platform. "My name is Jezebel."

Gianna paused, her mind a whirl of thoughts, "Jezebel. You were Queen of Israel, weren't you? The Bible says that you were eaten by dogs."

"I was the power and spirit behind that fool of a queen!" She growled; her agitation palpable. "Without me, she would have been just another sniveling, subservient wench doing the bidding of her husband." She began to pace back and forth as she emoted angrily. "I made Queen

Jezebel and King Ahab the infamous power team they turned out to be. Bringing Israel to its knees in service to Ba'al, The Great Darkness, raised my ranking to principality and made me more powerful than even the Prince of Persia!" Maniacal laughter.

Gianna prayed in her mind as Jezabel monologued.

When the laughter subsided, Gianna couldn't help but ask, "But you didn't have full victory. What about Elijah?"

Jezebel scowled, her eyes again like flames. "That fool, Ahab, let Elijah fall through his hands too many times to count!" Gianna winced at the angry outburst, "He should have killed him when he had the chance. We lost over 1,000 priests and prophets to that man and his God!" Jezabel's face relaxed back to a look of superior disgust, "But no matter, all of Israel still served The Great Darkness, fire from heaven or no." She began to chuckle again but was interrupted.

"Um, excuse me, did you say "all"? Weren't there 5,000 people who didn't bow to Baal?" Gianna had no clue why she kept provoking this woman or… thing. She was horrified when those words left her mouth, but they kept coming out as if by their own will.

The flames on the columns all around rose up, as did Jezebel's eyes.

"Oh, yes," she answered. "Our Enemy reserved for Himself 5,000, but to what purpose? We killed most of His prophets, and the people, His "chosen" ones, chose to serve The Great Darkness rather than Him. And now, I am about to be promoted again because my task is almost complete. I was given command over the most wicked warriors of hell." She gestured to a nearby column, "Lust!"

There amid the flame, a dark shadow pulsated and grew until it took the shape of a substantial, red, eight-armed lizard with three heads. It stood on hind legs, whipping around a pointed, knife-like tail, and its eight muscular arms ended in sharp talons. Its heads terrified Gianna. The one in the middle was like a dragon with dripping fangs and wicked black eyes. The right and left heads were human-like in form with disgustingly devilish features. One looked male with short, black hair, yellow eyes, and a long black tongue that slithered in and out of "his" mouth. The female head, also with black hair and yellow eyes, had crimson lips and blood dribbling down her mouth and chin.

Jezebel laughed at Gianna's obvious disgust. Then she shouted, "Pride!"

Lust disappeared, and another shadow grew into a form. This one appeared to be a hulking pig-faced creature whose body consisted of a muscular black human torso with the bottom half of a goat.

Before Gianna could process her revulsion, Jezebel shouted the next name, "Apathy!"

The swine demon fizzled away, and a tall humanoid creature appeared. Pale blue eyes stared into nothingness, albino white skin covered a naked, sexless body, and its lanky legs and arms looked usefully impossible. Gianna shivered at the sight, feeling cold and empty as despairing memories seeped into her thoughts. She closed her eyes for a second, praying she would wake up from this nightmare.

When she opened her eyes again, the albino was gone, and Jezebel grinned wildly at her. "Those beauties were just a few that I have on task to destroy marriages and families across the world." The witch's insane joy at atrocious evil reminded Gianna of Batman's nemesis, The Joker. Similarly, Jezebel was extremely animated in the emotional oration of her mania. "Our task is almost complete; the definition of marriage and family is ambiguous and subject to ever-shifting law. The internet and Hollywood have succeeded in mainstreaming pornography, fornication, adultery, and other delicious vices. All that's left is to tear each 'believing' family apart, piece by piece, for my master's pleasure." She threw her arms up like she'd just won a marathon, cackling madly.

Gianna glared at the witch in front of her, hating the thought of her life being picked apart for Satan's "pleasure." She could feel the anger burning in her belly, and it spread to her arms and hands. She pulled her sais out of her belt and clenched them tightly.

Jezebel suddenly stopped laughing and looked into Gianna's eyes, "Do you want to attack me, *girl?*" She sneered wickedly and tilted her head, doglike. "I wouldn't be so hasty."

She threw off her cloak and stepped forward into the firelight. Thick black tentacles emerged from either side of her body, wrapped tightly around two struggling human forms. The figure to Gianna's right emerged into the light. Gianna dropped the blades and gasped as she put her hand to her mouth.

"David?"

Diego, Darrel, Lincoln, and Lucy stood among the statues watching Gianna and Jezebel's interaction as the demonic woman boasted of her plans to destroy families. Lincoln had alerted the team that Gianna was no longer with them pretty soon after she had wandered off, and Diego had them backtrack to find her. They had come upon the two women shortly after that and had observed everything that transpired between Gianna and Jezebel. It seemed as with Lincoln that neither woman could see or hear them.

Billie Jean flew up to get a closer look at who the demon was holding captive in her slippery tentacles. The white eagle flew around Jezebel's head, squawking loudly, but the witch didn't even duck when she got inches from Jezebel's face. It was as if the eagle was a ghost.

She was on her own. Again, the group could only watch as one of them went up against a shrewd enemy. Diego immediately began to pray. Darrel, still unconvinced, stuck to fuming. Lucy felt ill-equipped for prayer but sent a quick "Please help Gianna!" up to heaven. Lincoln did a lot of praying as he paced around the statues, and Billie Jean continued her watch from above.

Gianna watched as Jezebel's tentacles wrapped tightly around her husband, with only his eyes exposed and wide with fear.

"Is this really David or some sick trick of this demon to mess with my mind?"

Jezebel giggled as she seemed to really enjoy this reveal.

"What do you want from me, witch?" Gianna furrowed her brows as her anger began to boil up at being toyed with by the beastly witch.

Jezebel laughed. "Silly child, only for you to finish what I started."

Immediately, she thrust the other black appendage forward into the light, which was wrapped around Alice. Gianna stepped back in surprise, the familiar pain flashing through her chest and stomach, causing her to stagger slightly. Her eyes began to tear up, so she closed them and took a deep breath, willing herself to control her feelings.

Inside, she whimpered weakly. *Oh, Papa, I can't do this.*

The soft reply came. *My daughter, I am with you.*

I'm going to fail. Gianna pleaded.

No. You will rise.

Gianna opened her eyes and saw Jezebel cackling again, but thankfully she began to block out the obnoxious noise. Meanwhile, her former friend and her husband's mistress trembled. And though her mouth was also covered, tears slid down her pale face.

"Gianna, are you pleased to see your rival in my possession?"

She didn't answer.

"Well, let me inform you," she purred, "that I took them as they were in the very act of betrayal. They seemed to be really enjoying themselves, too. Shall I describe it to you?" Jezebel asked eagerly.

Gianna gritted her teeth. "Enough! Let them go and fight me instead!"

"Come closer, girl!" Jezebel snapped her fingers.

Suddenly, Gianna was directly in front of Jezebel, her helpless victims now facing her on the platform as the monster towered over her slight 5'3" frame. The atmosphere was oppressive, making it hard to stand up straight—as if an immense, invisible hand was pushing down on her. Jezebel's fangs gleamed brightly as she held David and Alice up like trophies.

"All you have to do is say the word, and I could squeeze the life out of them right now."

"No!" shouted Gianna, as the vicious mix of emotions

began to flare like a fire in her belly. "Take me! Fight me!"

"Oh Gianna, just think about what they've done. The utter betrayal. Tearing both families apart. Think of how they humiliated you." David and Alice's eyes were pleading with unspoken fervency as Jezebel continued, "It would be so easy to be done with both of them . . ."

Instantly, thoughts and memories filled Gianna's mind of the past few months: David getting home late every night from work "meetings," their son, Dylan, asking for him as she put him to bed before his dad got home.

She remembered how Alice brought her son over for playdates every week and how concerned she acted when Gianna confided in her about David's strange behavior, his long phone conversations outside in the driveway, and Gianna's prayers for their marriage as she felt the distance between them widen.

Gianna saw the text messages between David and Alice after looking through his phone while he was in the shower. The fresh memory of the confrontation where he confessed, he had been having sex with Alice for months while still coming home to be with Gianna. At that moment, the lies, manipulation, and pain consumed her as strongly as they did the first time.

The anger, hate, and hurt were a giant ball in her chest as she relived how she had insisted he get out. But instead, he began to beg her for another chance to be a better man. David claimed that he would end the affair, he wanted to end it, but he didn't know how.

She had burned with hatred for him, remembering the words she'd spoken out of grief. "Why end it, David? Go enjoy her. You've destroyed two families with abandon, why stop now? Does her husband know? No? Maybe he should! He's a hunter, right, with lots of guns? He'd probably like to know his friend is nailing his wife! You should run away with her and make a nice life of two deceiving, manipulating bastards and raise some little bastard kids while you're at it!"

He eventually left, but he continued to come by the house, and the pain in her stomach intensified. She stopped eating and dined on bitterness and anger. She lay on the floor night after night and wept before the Lord, asking Him to free her and take her home.

Why me, Lord? Why? I loved him. I was a faithful wife and mother. Why?

Then it was all she could do to endure his infernal begging for forgiveness. She despised him, though, and the hate became like a dark hole in her chest.

She hated them both, but she didn't want them to die; *she* wanted to die. The thoughts and memories washed over Gianna like waves, and her heart felt each pain like it was new again—stabbing, stabbing, stabbing pain. She was drowning in a whirlwind of feelings and memories.

"That's right, Gianna, you feel that agony. Who hurts someone they love like that?" The wicked voice seemed far away. She clenched her teeth to keep her from screaming and opened her stinging eyes to look at her enemies: that grinning, monstrous Jezebel, her husband, and his mistress.

"Yessssss!" Jezebel cackled. "Look at ussssss, *your en-emies.*"

Gianna was shaking as she reached down to grab her weapons. Her breathing was erratic, her heartbeat wild, the wound in her heart throbbing viciously.

"Free yourself, Gianna, let me squeeze the life out of these, the source of your pain, and then you can kill me, for I was the author of all of it! My minions feverishly worked to draw him away, putting thoughts in her mind of ways to entice him, creating opportunities for them to be together…Yesss!" Jezebel fell into a fit of laughter.

Gianna groaned. How tempting to allow them to suffer and to feel horror. She knelt there, thinking.

If they died here, would they really be dead? It may still be a dream. It may not even really be them.

She knew deep down that she must overcome here. This was her battle. How was she to win? Yet, she was so gripped by her hate and her pain. She looked at Alice, who had tears streaming down her face, whimpering beneath Jezebel's grip.

Gianna felt no compassion for her. She felt nothing. Then she looked at her husband, his sad eyes pleading with her. He disgusted her. His eyes were the same way when he was begging for her forgiveness. For a moment, Gianna wondered if she could walk away and leave them both with this fiend.

In the distance, there was a lightning flash. Instantly, Gianna was at the foot of a cross on a gray mountain with a black sky and lightning flashes overhead. She caught her breath in disbelief and kept looking. At the base of the cross was a pool of blood and further up, broken, bleeding feet nailed hard into the splintered, thick wood.

She reached her shaking hand up to touch the precious feet, her gaze traveling up the torn and bloody legs, and then fully beholding the naked, battered body of the Innocent One nailed to the rough beams. His chest rose and fell shallowly and quickly as He struggled to breathe. His face, a mess of blood and broken bone, hardly looked human. The Lord looked down at her with eyes of such deep love, it hurt her to see it and gasping as she quickly realized that she was holding a bloody hammer and nails. Screaming in shock, she threw the tools down. Then the raspy whisper of a voice spoke, "Father . . . forgive her, for she knows not what she's doing."

Gianna's heart broke. She fell at the foot of the cross that held her Precious Friend. She laid down in the pool of His blood and wept.

"My Lord! My Lord! I'm so sorry! Please forgive me!"

"Forgive them, child," His whisper came in her ear.

She looked, and He was kneeling beside her, but He was now whole and so beautiful. He touched her face, her broken heart became full, and she felt it would burst with His love. There was no hate or anger in His presence, nor any pain or sorrow.

Gianna reached her hand to Him, and He scooped her up as a father to his newborn baby, holding her to His chest.

"I'm sorry, Master. I forgive them." She sobbed, clinging to him. "Please take the hurt and hate, I don't want it. Save me!"

"Precious daughter, I bore it for you on the cross, and that's where it is and where it will stay."

She began to calm as she looked in His eyes, "Can I stay with you?"

He gently wiped her tears, "No, child. You must go back and complete your destiny. But I am always with you, Gianna."

"Please. Please . . ." She moaned. "Do I have to go back to that awful place? I don't know how to beat Jezebel."

Again, He touched her face strengthening her, "You already have. Open your eyes, daughter."

Immediately, she was back on the platform. She felt strengthened from her encounter with Jesus. She looked at David and Alice again, and the hate and disgust were gone, replaced with the knowledge of her true enemy. She glared at Jezebel, who had stopped laughing and now had fear in her eyes. Gianna had no fear, for she felt Him with her.

"Put them down, devil!" she commanded as she crouched low with her blades in hand.

David and Alice disappeared in a puff of smoke. Jezebel growled and opened her mouth wide, displaying now lengthened fangs. For the ultimate display of intimidation, she threw her shoulders back to accentuate her seven-foot frame, and her tentacles splayed wildly behind her. Yet, Gianna's gaze was unmoved and calm; to her, the demon looked weak and defenseless.

She felt the power begin to flow through her arms, and she attacked Jezebel with remarkable speed. Every move the fiend made seemed to come in slow motion, and she was stunned at the ease with which she blocked and parried the blows from the tentacles and razor-sharp nails of the witch. Within what seemed like a few effortless minutes, Gianna stood over her dead enemy, one of the blades embedded into the demon queen's forehead, and several severed tentacles scattered around the writhing corpse. Gianna shivered with disgust at the sight.

As she freed her blade from the corpse, Billie Jean's eagle cry came from above. The giant white eagle landed and walked towards her, transforming into a beautiful goddess as she quickly embraced Gianna warmly. Like sunshine breaking through rain clouds, Gianna enjoyed every second of being smashed into a group hug with these new friends that she surprisingly cared so much for in such a short time. The joy was palpable.

CHAPTER 6

The team shouted in joy as they left behind the dark forest with its many trials. They were greeted by an open sky bursting with orange and pink patterns. The sun slowly retreated behind the great mountain in front of them. Diego suggested they make camp in an area where they could keep a clear watch. Within a few yards of the great mountain, they found a grassy space with a few surrounding trees. Soon, Lincoln and Darrel had a fire going, and they all settled around it.

Gianna watched the flames of the campfire dance as her mind played out the day's events, and Jezebel's raucous laugh rang in her ears. Lucy sat close to her, and she felt the young girl's small frame shiver. Instinctively, Gianna put her arm around Lucy and pulled her close as she would with her own child. Her mind drifted to thinking of her son, and Gianna ached to hold him. She quickly pushed the thought away, unwilling to feel sadness after the triumph of her victory.

They all were lying or sitting around the fire. Lincoln was already asleep in his cloak. Billie and Darrel listened intently to the professor's answers to Darrel's unending questions. She and Lucy sat drawn together by something Gianna was still trying to figure out. The dark-haired teen had stopped shivering and had her hands up to the fire, arms outstretched, dozens of line-thin scars on her forearms now painfully visible in the firelight. Gianna reached out and ran her finger lightly over the scars on one of Lucy's arms.

"Tell me why you hurt yourself," she said quietly.

Lucy quickly pulled her arms under her cloak and answered, still looking at the flames. "You don't expect it to be something that's addicting, and every time you do it, you hate it, and you hate yourself. Then you wake up in the morning and realize your sheets are bloody." Tears began to slide down her face. "You didn't even know you were doing it."

Lucy cried silently against Gianna, but her body shook with sobs. Gianna held her close and, through her own tears, asked, "But why? Why do you do it?"

Wiping her face with her cloak, Lucy sat up and clutched it to herself like a security blanket, "At first it's like a release. Like the pain in your heart and mind is too much, and when you cut yourself, it seems to go away a little."

Gianna wiped a stray tear from Lucy's cheek, "What

happened, dear? What pain are you trying to get relief from?"

Lucy looked down, "My dad left me and my mom when I was five, but my mom never got over him, ya' know? She just kept sleeping with all these guys to try to forget him, I guess. Sometimes they would stick around our apartment for a while and, like, freeload off my mom. And sometimes she'd go to work and let them watch me."

She looked around at the others cautiously, to confirm that only Gianna could hear. "The first guy, Carlos, started to touch me and stuff. Then he would buy me candy and toys to keep my mouth shut. But, after a few times, he really started to scare me and wanted to do more and more each time. I'm only, like, six years old, ya know?" Lucy paused, biting her bottom lip and, still staring into the fire, she continued, "So, I tell my mom, and she throws the guy out cursing and screaming, but then she yells at me too and starts to tell me that it's my fault. That I run around in my underwear too much. I'm just crying, ya know?"

Gianna nodded and moved a stray hair back behind Lucy's ear. Lucy took a breath, "Well, it was a while before another guy stayed, but she started the same crap and let him babysit me . . ." She shook her head and shrugged,

"I just stopped telling her when they touched me. Then it just kept happening with different guys. I can't even tell you how many and of course a few of 'em didn't stop at just touching. They raped me. She'd catch 'em sometimes touching me or something, and she'd get rid of 'em. She started calling me 'puta' (whore), ya' know? I think I went numb after a while; I couldn't eat and started cutting."

Gianna's tears fell in sympathy for Lucy, wondering why such horrible things happened to her in her short life. At the same time, anger boiled in her chest at a mom who didn't love and protect her daughter and at the monsters who preyed on innocent children. She wanted to find a way to get Lucy out of her home situation when this crazy adventure was over. As the young girl drifted to sleep next to her, Gianna stroked her hair, but could not find rest herself as she prayed and planned. After her victory against Jezebel, she felt like the weight of the world had been lifted from her shoulders. Now a new burden settled that she hadn't anticipated, and she began to talk to the Lord about it. The whispered assurance of the Holy Spirit soon came.

Peace, Daughter. Rest now, I have already taken care of this.

Gianna smiled, and soon her mind drifted to the memory of being in the Lord's arms and His eyes that were so full of love. As she watched the night sky begin to lighten, Gianna finally drifted into sleep with the warmth of that memory still lingering at the edges of her dreams.

They each took turns on watch while the others slept—and they slept hard; exhaustion from the day's events mixed with relief of finally being free from the forest both taking their toll. Sometime after the fourth watch, the wind shifted, and the last embers of the fire crackled and went out. Lucy turned over and woke with a start out of a troubling dream. She rubbed her eyes and looked at the others to see who was on watch. Billie Jean chirped lightly from the tree above her and tilted her head to focus one eagle eye on Lucy. The girl stood up and whispered, "I'm going to use the bathroom." Billie Jean chirped again approvingly.

Lucy walked toward the sporadic growth of evergreens at the base of Mount Joy, a few yards away. She could see more than she thought as the edges of dawn crept up behind the hills and cast an eerie yellow-gray light over the land.

"Dawn. The time between times," she whispered to herself.

She found a pine with a thick trunk surrounded by

foliage to do her business behind. Once finished, as she secured her cloak, a large black bird landed on a branch directly above and stared.

"You're a big nosy bird, aren't you?" she asked and then giggled nervously to herself.

"Nevermore!" the bird answered.

Lucy jumped back, "Did you just talk?"

"Nevermore!" The bird squawked again.

Lucy rubbed her eyes and pinched her face, "I must be dreaming!"

The big black bird stared at Lucy more intently and said, "Nevermore!"

Then it fluttered off to the next tree and stared at her again, before flying a bit further.

"I think you must want me to follow you," she said to the bird.

The bird fluttered from tree to tree towards the mountain, and Lucy followed, feeling both curious and nervous about where it would lead her. Soon, she was led to a dirt path going up the mountain base. The raven continued its flutter, jumping from bush to tree, slowly coaxing her forward with its knowing stare and one-word vocabulary of

NEVERMORE.

All of a sudden, Lucy saw a young man running down the path toward her, shouting, "Help! Help! Please!"

She ran towards him, and, as she got closer, Lucy saw that he was bleeding from the stomach, holding one hand over his wound and waving her down with the other. The boy looked familiar, but as she came face to face with him, she was shocked that she knew him.

"Kevin?!"

Kevin was a boy that she used to hang out with from her school. It had been a while since they last spoke because he and his group had decided Lucy wasn't welcome amongst them anymore.

"Kevin, what happened?" she reached out to him tentatively as she tried to assess if he was real.

He was deathly pale, and his eyes were wide with terror as he kept glancing behind. He started to lean on her, and she put her arm around his back. He felt real.

"Crystal and I went into a cave up there for shelter," he said. "And there was this creepy old guy, he said his name was Despair. He invited us in to stay the night—"

"Crystal's here too?! Where is she?"

"She's still in the cave. I . . . I think she's dead. . ." He looked down and moaned, "We gotta' get outta' here! Now! He could be coming!"

"Wait, are you sure she's dead? Could she still be alive? I have to go after her!"

"I don't know! I don't know! She cut herself pretty bad! There was so much blood. Oooooo . . . we gotta' get outa' here!" He started to walk forward on his own, but only stumbled a few feet away.

Lucy went to him and helped ease him to the ground, propping him up against a large rock. "Kevin, you need to sit here! I'm going to make sure Crystal doesn't need help. I'll be right back."

"Wait, Lucy!" He grabbed her arm. "That old guy, he's crazy! Don't listen to him! He tries to convince you to kill yourself. That's what Crystal did; I tried to stop her. I tried to—but she cut me and told me to shut up. Then she sliced both her wrists." Kevin covered his face and began to weep.

Clenching her fists, Lucy felt power course through her body, "Stay here, Kevin. I'll be back." She started quickly towards the cave.

Up ahead, the raven had begun squawking loudly from

atop a large rock sitting on the same path from which Kevin had just come. When she came into sight, the bird stopped its noisy ruckus and stared at her. She put her hands on her hips and glared at it, "Okay, you crazy bird, let's go!" It flitted off, and she followed.

After some time, the raven turned a bend and seemed to disappear. As Lucy came around the same curve, she suddenly lurched back with a scream of terror caught in her throat. She had barely missed colliding with a dead body hanging from the tree in front of her.

The teenage boy's bloated face and mouth, frozen in agony, sent a shiver of revulsion down her spine. As she slowly broke her gaze from the boy, she realized that every tree leading up to the dark, gaping cave had bodies suspended from sporadic branches. A putrid-smelling breeze kept the corpses in constant sway as men and women, old and young, with frozen blue death masks silently stared into oblivion.

Feeling light-headed, Lucy's vision threatened to fade. Her breathing shortened, and her chest ached with the strain of trying to catch her breath. She found a patch of grass and collapsed to her knees, dry heaving until she vomited. She grasped the edge of her cloak and wiped her mouth, gradually able to take deeper breaths. After a bit, she decided to continue on and closed her eyes, whispering a quick prayer. She then stood up slowly, her vision crisp and turned back toward the cave mouth.

My God, what am I doing here? Lucy thought as she stared into the darkness.

"Nevermore!" squawked the raven from the cave entrance.

It flew into the cave. Lucy, thinking about Crystal, took a deep breath and followed it inside.

Billie Jean gently shook Gianna awake. Gianna opened her eyes and sat up quickly,

"What? Are we going?"

"I can't find Lucy." Billie Jean whispered, her eyebrows knit with worry.

"Are you sure? Did you see her leave?" Gianna quickly stood up and strapped on her blades.

"Yes, I was watching from the trees near camp when she woke up a little bit ago and said she had to pee. I watched her go to some bushes a little ways off, and she never came back." Billie Jean pointed to the area. "I went over there and flew around to look nearby, but she disappeared."

"Lucy wouldn't go anywhere without telling us, would she?"

"I don't know, but come with me. Let's see if we can find her." Billie Jean answered.

Gianna looked over at the sleeping men and bent down to rouse Lincoln.

He opened one eye, "Is it my turn for the watch?" he asked groggily.

"Yes, Lincoln. Listen, Billie and I are going to check on Lucy. We think she may have wandered off."

He sat up, concern for Lucy knocking the sleep right off. "Let's wake the others, and we'll all go look."

Gianna shook her head, "No, if we find her right away, I would feel bad waking them. Billie will fly back to get you if we need you, ok?"

He stood up, nodded, and strapped his sword on, "Okay, I'll be watching for you, but if you're gone too long, I'm going to wake them up and come after you."

"Got it."

With that, Gianna and Billie Jean jogged off towards

the area where Lucy was last seen.

Lucy stood inside the entrance as her eyes adjusted to the dim enclosure; the cave was gloomy and smelled worse than a dumpster. She attempted to breathe shallowly through her mouth to keep the worst of the stench at bay.

The entrance was narrow but soon began to widen further in. Torches lined the walls at intervals, throwing flickering light and shadow on several of the interior surfaces. Lucy noted the absence of the raven, as she stepped cautiously through a dark puddle covering most of the floor, shivering as her boot steps grew slow and thick with the substance now clinging to the bottoms of them.

As she turned a corner, she suddenly jumped back, stifling a scream as she almost stepped on two bodies lying on the ground across the path in front of her. A young man and woman, not much older than herself, were entwined in an embrace. They looked asleep, except no movement or sound escaped from them.

A "tsssking" sound interrupted her terror as a robed man stepped out of the shadows, shaking his head.

"What a shame... they were forbidden to be together in

life due to a family dispute, so they chose to be together in death. I'm sure they're happy, reunited in the paradise for lovers."

The man was old, with a thin white beard and long greasy, unkempt hair. Lucy was repelled at first, knowing this was the man named Despair that Kevin had warned her about, but soon she found that his voice was somewhat soothing.

"I've been expecting you, Lucy," his sickly-sweet voice seemed to calm her edginess.

"You have?" Lucy said, her mind beginning to feel a bit foggy.

She came here with an urgent purpose but was having a hard time remembering what that was.

"Why, of course, I have. Come in. Let me get you some refreshment." He walked further into the cave, and Lucy followed.

What was it? Why had she come here? How did he know her? He seemed so familiar, but she couldn't place him. The bottoms of her boots clung to the sticky floor as she walked, causing her to shiver with disgust. The air inside the cave seemed to thicken with the metallic smell of blood. As they continued walking, Lucy observed more bodies scattered here and there on the ground, some with empty cups tipped near them, and others with knives in their hands, lying in dark pools of blood.

As she continued to follow Despair further into the stifling darkness, Lucy felt strangely numb to the macabre scene; her thoughts were muddled but striving for clarity. In vain, she tried to remember something important; her stomach clenched with urgency, and her heart beat fast in her ears. The old man turned back toward her, pushing a cup into her hand.

"It's spiced wine," he smiled, an odd gesture that didn't match his face. "It will ease your nerves and clear your mind."

How nice of him. I do need help clearing my mind.

But her insides still felt cold and twisted.

She held the cup and sniffed, smelling cinnamon and berries. Suddenly, she was parched, as if she hadn't had a drink in days. She took a cautious sip and found that it was tasty, but it burned in her throat and chest as it went down. She coughed, spattering some of the drink on the floor. And despite her best wishes, her head only felt cloudier.

"I'm looking for someone," Lucy muttered with confusion. Her voice sounded detached from her mouth. She didn't even know why she said it until it came out. "Yes!" she said louder. "I'm looking for someone!" But now her voice sounded as if it were coming from the walls.

Why was it doing that?

"Oh? And who would that be, Lucy?" He inched closer to her.

"Wait. How do you know me?" She asked, straining to focus on the strange man's face.

"Oh, I know all about you, Lucy Ortiz." He tssked again and shook his head. "So sad, really, how your mother neglected you and turned her head as her boyfriends took advantage of you, a defenseless little girl." She nodded and handed him back the cup, sudden sadness coming over her. "Then she even blamed you when the relationships didn't work. And you, poor dear, with no father to love and defend you! See, I know. I know how hard you've had it." He patted her back like a trusted friend.

Again, his voice soothed but also scared her. Unbidden tears began to escape her eyes, and images from her childhood played like a movie in her head. She felt the gaping hole in her heart for a mother and a father's love, as if it were a fresh wound.

"Oh, dear. Yes, I know the ache," he tsked again as he

shook his head. "Then the difficulty of fitting in at school. The friends who would come and go. Oh, and that little group of kids who finally accepted you. . . until they decided you weren't *really* one of them."

By this time, Lucy shook with sobs as the rejection hit her all over again. She vaguely noted that urgency again in her gut when he mentioned the kids: Kevin, Crystal, and the others who had snubbed and dismissed her as if they never knew her. . .

Oh, no! Kevin!

Through her tears, she managed to choke out, "Kevin. . . Crystal? Where is Crystal?"

"Who?"

"I'm looking for Crystal . . ." she raked her sleeve across her wet nose and face.

He shook his head. "I'm sorry, Lucy . . . Did you say, Crystal? Wasn't she the one who told you to kill yourself after her boyfriend began flirting with you?"

Franko came crashing into her mind. For weeks he would catch her in the hall on her way to math and again after health class at the end of the day. But she never liked him and always felt creeped out by his attention. She backed away when he tried to kiss her one day, but he called her a prude and stalked away furiously.

The next day, the whole group walked away from her when she tried to join them in the hall before school started. Later on, in the bathroom, Crystal pushed Lucy against the wall and accused her of trying to go for Franko. Lucy denied it and tried to explain, but the girls cursed her out, told her to go home, and kill herself. Lucy crumpled on the floor in tears.

"Oh, dear Lucy. That pain is so hard to live with." Despair placed his hand on his chest, "It hurts so much, doesn't it? How long can it keep feeling that way? Life is so painful."

Lucy nodded as she felt the pain settle like an enormous weight in her chest, and she hated it.

"Life, for you, has been nothing but one pain after another. Life has been so cruel to you," he continued. "What if it just continues to be one disappointment, rejection, and sorrow after another? What kind of life is that for someone to live? If only there was a way to make the pain stop."

She nodded in agreement as stray tears dripped off her cheeks.

Oh yes, if it would just stop...

"It *can* stop, dear girl." He took a small dagger from his belt and put it in her hand. She held the knife, turning it over in her hand and feeling the familiar draw to release the inner ache. She contemplated the end of pain.

Lucy. Remember Love. My Love.

It was a flash of a thought...the words, not her own. And another memory came to her. She saw herself at 9 years old, at a vacation bible school with her friend, Amy, who'd lived next door. They had so much fun, singing songs and watching skits about Jesus. She really loved the stories and new friends. The teacher talked to them about what it meant to invite Jesus to come live in their hearts. She had asked Jesus to come into her heart that day, and she had a dream that same night that she was sitting on the Lord's lap. Looking into her eyes, He had said, "Lucy, you're mine now. I love you, and I will never let you go. I will always be with you." He then hugged her tight to himself. Lucy woke up that morning and had felt like she really had been with Jesus, and she cried tears of happiness. The memory flooded her with joy as if it had just happened. She felt His presence with her in the dark cave.

I remember now, Lord.

Instantly that aching hole of rejection felt full of His

love, and the pain fled. She opened her eyes and declared, "I remember, Jesus! I AM LOVED!"

Despair's eyes grew wide with horror as she said those words. Suddenly, Lucy's whole body began to glow, and she felt power fill and flow through her as she shouted again, "I AM LOVED!"

Incredible light and energy filled the cave, and the old man screamed with terror as illuminated power pierced through his body.

His face began to distort and change shape, first into a grotesque black-eyed demon, then morphing into Kevin's face and back to his original visage. Despair screamed in terror as the searing light penetrated him, and his face began to crack like a porcelain plate. Lucy watched in amazed shock as the resulting explosion seemed to dissolve him and every other dark and dead object within its radius.

Meanwhile, Billie Jean and Gianna followed the path they thought Lucy had been on when they heard an explosion nearby, which seemed to shake the whole mountain. Gianna screamed in fear, "Oh no! Lucy!!" She ran up the path, worried at what she would find. Before long, she spotted a large cave. Billie Jean landed beside her, instantly changing back into her human form. As they came upon the cave entrance, they noticed a skeleton in a monk's robe lying on the ground just outside.

Gianna touched it with her boot, and a knife fell from its hand. She shivered.

"Could this be where the explosion came from? I don't see anything charred or any blasted rock."

"No, this can't be it. Lucy!" Billie Jean called out. "Lucy, are you up here?"

A faint voice responded from inside the cave, "I'm in here."

They ran inside and found her standing alone in the middle of an empty cave. Relieved, they embraced her.

Gianna pulled back, looking into the girl's face, "Lucy, are you okay?"

Lucy responded with a wide smile, nodding, "Yes. I'm really, really okay."

"What happened?"

Lucy looked around at the empty cave, still in wonder at what had just taken place. There were no bodies, no blood, not even the smell of death.

"I...I really don't know. It's so crazy, but I'm better."

She smiled and stood up straighter. "I remembered something really important that I had forgotten. Let's get out of this gross place, I have to tell you all about it."

After the girls returned, Lucy caught everyone up on what had taken place. Her victory was apparent in her bright countenance and joyful animation as she related the tale. Darrel high-fived her and told her how impressed he was by her explosion power. "I definitely need to see that in person, Little LuLu!" He laughed.

She shrugged, "I don't know how I did it, though!" They all laughed at that.

Lincoln hugged her, "I'm so glad you made it back safely, Lucy."

Diego beamed, "I'm very proud of you, hija!"

Before long, the morning had warmed up, and the team set out to climb the mountain together, encouraged by Lucy's victory. Diego led them forward with Lucy beside him, chatting away about her experience as their banter created a light and uplifting mood. Not too far behind, Gianna, Lincoln, and Darrel made small talk as Billie Jean uncharacteristically started the trek in her human form.

CHAPTER 7

Diego encouraged them onward as the group slowly made their way up the rough terrain of Mount Joy. The main path became steep and rocky, and they stopped a few times to catch their breath, the air getting thinner as they ascended. Billie Jean transformed into a lion shortly after the first part of the trek, separating herself from the rest by trotting to the lead. Lucy jogged ahead, catching up to her a bit later, and casually asked if she was going to stay in animal form the whole way up.

"Most likely," Billie Jean said flatly. "Why?"

"I dunno," Lucy shrugged. "It's, like, hard to really get to know the real you when you're a lion or an eagle. It's weird that we've been through all this stuff together and I've never really talked to you. . . I mean, to your real face, ya' know?"

"Well . . . that's not my real face either," Billie Jean answered dismissively, pausing to change into an eagle and fly off high above the team.

She scanned the rocky, rough mountain, then the valley below, her vision sharp and able to spot a rabbit in the brush, and even further down, a field mouse raced for cover. Billie Jean stretched her wings and glided on the wind, enjoying every aspect of her new abilities. Her mind drifted back to her conversation with Lucy.

No one here really knew her, and she liked that. In fact, she loved not being the Billie Jean of the "real world." What if this was real and that other world the dream? Then she really could be the beauty, the lion, and the eagle and that other depressed, lonely, fat girl no one noticed would be the dream. Billie Jean wanted that other girl and her pain to fade away forever.

Sudden movement in the sky ahead snapped her from her dark thoughts. Large, black, winged figures flew towards them rapidly, and Billie Jean quickly called out a warning to the others below. Gianna and the others looked up when they heard her. Lincoln pointed to the cloud of winged creatures heading towards them, "Look! Something's coming! Get ready!"

The path wasn't wide enough for them to circle up, so they stood back to back in pairs. Lucy and Gianna paired up, just as Gianna's arms began to tingle with power. She quickly withdrew her blades, her heart pumping wildly.

"Lucy, can you shield us?" she asked.

"I. .I'll try," Lucy stammered.

"I know you can do it, Lucy. Don't freak out, just breathe and ask God to help you."

Lucy nodded, her eyebrows furrowed with nervous energy.

Darrel and Lincoln were also back to back: Darrel with his arms flamed up and ready, while Lincoln began to strike his sword loudly against his shield, screaming, "LET'S GO!"

Diego, close by with his staff glowing, prayed for angelic protection and supernatural strength. The hairs on the back of their necks stood up as the hellish screams of the creatures filled the sky just as they descended. He could finally see what was coming and recognized them immediately. He never imagined meeting such a creature face to face.

The harpies had the heads and torsos of women, gaping maws filled with razor-sharp fangs, and the wings, legs, and clawed feet of rapacious vultures.

Diego cried out, "Animo peregrinos! Courage, Pilgrims! They feed on fear! Be strong in the Lord, and we will overcome them!"

Billie Jean's eagle cry resounded loudly as she launched toward the first of them with her large talons and beak. The fiend screamed and fell back, and she quickly tore into another one.

Billie Jean's actions were all the group needed to spur them forward. They shouted a battle cry and began attacking the black brood.

Darrel's flames were able to overwhelm two or three foes at a time; they would fall, but more would quickly take their place. Gianna and Lincoln stabbed and sliced, and as they did, wings, legs, claws, and even heads dropped everywhere. Half a dozen harpies came at them at once, and Lucy released a wave of power that sent the creatures sprawling backward, squalling in pain.

Diego shot blasts of glory light from his staff at one, then another, and they fell left and right. Soon, black harpy corpses littered the path all around them and the valley below, but more kept coming. The team was wearying quickly.

Billie Jean soon began to sustain many bites and tears. She was tired and bleeding but still kept fighting. She had no choice. Yet, the adrenaline and intense battle energy were waning, and she began to wonder if she would make it. This battle would be her undoing if the vicious hags didn't stop coming.

For the first time since waking up in this strange world, she prayed, "Lord, if You're listening, please help us. I don't want to die in this place."

At once, a wondrous sound came from above, altogether like a lion's deep roar mixed with an eagle's scream that resonated across the sky. Whatever it was, it terrified the harpies, and they began to scatter in different directions.

Like lightning, a great golden Gryphon appeared. It was an enormous creature with the body and hindquarters of a lion, and head, front claws, and wings of an eagle. It swooped in and grabbed three harpies in each claw, and, with its giant beak, tore them apart, the pieces falling into the valley below. Then, turning, it came back for more.

The warriors watched in wonder, mouths agape. In what seemed like mere seconds, all the harpies were dead; not one escaped. Thereafter, the majestic lion-eagle roar resounded again. The team looked at the distinguished creature in awe.

For a moment, the Gryphon flapped its great golden wings and hovered just above them. Its eyes were like blue gemstones that glistened incredibly in the light. It looked intently at Billie Jean, who was flapping nearby; she gazed back at it in wonder.

Then, almost before they could blink, it grabbed her in one massive claw and flew off.

"Nooooo!" Darrel cried out, shooting fire at the beast. But it was futile. The Gryphon was already miles away.

Diego put his hand on Darrel's chest, "Son, there is nothing you can do. If that creature was evil, it would not have saved us from the attack. It easily could've killed us all. Billie Jean will be back; trust me."

CHAPTER 8

Billie Jean tried in vain to free herself from the Gryphon's claw. She had transformed into her lion form to try biting and scratching, but she didn't succeed in leaving even a mark. Too exhausted from the fight with the harpies, she soon stopped struggling and turned back into human form.

Rest, she heard in her head.

Billie Jean looked up at the creature and found that it was gazing at her with one of its big jeweled eyes. At the same moment, she realized its grip was gentle and had never been tight or grasping. It turned its face back to the sky and continued to flap its great glistening wings.

Relenting, she laid back in the large claws as a refreshing cool wind blew over her aching, sweaty body. The sound of the Gryphon's wings beat a natural soothing rhythm, and her chattering thoughts soon dissipated. She gazed at the landscape far below, vast green forests and plains peaked through the wispy white clouds, and she wondered if they would fly on forever. She didn't really care if they did, actually, and even welcomed that prospect as her eyes closed, and she drifted into exhausted oblivion.

She awakened as she was gently laid on soft heather next to a crystal blue lake.

Drink, she heard the voice say softly in her head.

Billie Jean arose painfully, still feeling the ache of the fight in her bones and the sting of the gashes in her skin. The Gryphon stood by and watched silently as she waded carefully into the beautiful waters. She gasped when the frigid liquid hit her legs, feeling the goosebumps prickle up her skin. She dove under and came up drinking the cool, sweet water. It energized her as it hit her stomach, and she felt a powerful warmth that rippled across her body in waves. Suddenly, as she watched, all her scratches and gashes closed up and disappeared, and surprisingly, the aches in her muscles faded as well. She swam and paddled, enjoying the freedom from danger or worry, and like a child, immersed herself in the blissful beauty of her surroundings.

After floating idly for a while, she remembered the Gryphon. It was sitting by the water's edge, calmly watching her. When their eyes connected, Billie Jean immediately felt the Gryphon's joy in being present with her and felt its heart of pure love. Love for her. She thought her own heart would burst with the experience of it. In the midst of this shower of perfect love, she understood what it was— *who* it was. Love Himself.

The Waking

Suddenly, the Gryphon clawed the dirt and let out its powerful sky-filling call. The ground shook with its strange mix of a lion's roar and eagle's cry, and soon the Gryphon shot like a rocket into the clouds.

Billie Jean's heart skipped, and she caught her breath. As quickly as He flew off, she transformed and went after Him.

She called out an eagle cry and screamed, "Don't go!" But the great beast's wings were easily four times the size of her own, and He was yards ahead of her in an instant. She beat her wings in furious pursuit and called out again, "Don't go! Don't leave me!"

She flew and flew, but He never seemed closer. Her heart ached, and tears streamed from her eyes, clouding her sharp eagle vision. She began to tire in the pursuit and was close to giving up when she heard, *Don't stop, dear one.*

Billie Jean beat her wings even harder, and sure enough, she began to gain on Him. Was she actually catching up, or was He slowing down?

Meanwhile, Diego and the team were regrouping after

the battle. Gianna turned to Diego, "What should we do? Should we wait for her or keep going?"

Diego closed his eyes briefly. "We go on," he replied.

"Professor," Lucy's voice cracked weakly, "I'm so tired and thirsty. Can we wait here a while before we go on?"

Diego side-hugged her and shook his head, "I'm sorry, hija, we mustn't stop." He addressed the others, "We must try to get to the top before nightfall. We can make it if we keep steady on and don't stop too much."

None of them moved right away until Lincoln, who had been sitting cleaning black harpy blood off his sword, stood up with a small grunt. "All right, team, you heard Diego! Let's move!" He sheathed his sword and forced a smile.

No one else said anything, but a couple sighs, and groans were heard as they followed Diego and Lincoln slowly up the mountain. The top looked very far from where they were.

"Momma! Hurry up, Momma! Come on, catch us!"

Billie Jean's heart quickened.

Impossible! That couldn't be coming from the Gryphon?

Yet, the unmistakably familiar giggle came again from the Gryphon ahead of her.

Billie Jean sped up and focused her keen eyes and ears on the creature. And there, on its back, sat a little girl. The girl turned to look at her, smiling and waving as if on a merry-go-round at the mall.

Katie?

Immediately, Billie Jean sped up with power from somewhere only desperate mothers find.

KATIE.

Her heart continued to scream her daughter's name, and tears again flew like rain from her eyes, temporarily blurring her vision. She shook them away in frustration and flew and flew to get to that Gryphon and her baby girl . . . her dead baby girl!

How is this possible?

Just as she got close enough to almost touch her, the Gryphon began to descend. And Katie's lovely giggle came again.

"You almost got us! Come on, Momma!"

The clouds parted, and a place of remarkable beauty came into view. Green rolling hills and cliffs that overlooked rippling clear, jade waters. Trees of every color possible and even colors that a tree couldn't possibly be were growing there: purple tree trunks with rainbow leaves, yellow, orange, and shades she'd never seen before. The fragrance was exhilarating.

As the ground came into view, there appeared to be a couple dozen children running around and climbing the colorful trees. They waved and shouted as they saw the Gryphon coming towards them.

The Gryphon landed, and the children, of all races and ages, rushed over and climbed on Him. Katie got down and ran to her mother. Billie Jean had changed back to her human form as soon as she touched the ground, and she held her arms open as her knees hit the grass. The little girl ran into her embrace, and Billie Jean wept, planting thousands of kisses all over her daughter's face.

"Oh, Katie! Katie! Is it really you?"

Katie put her little hand on her mother's face, "It's me, Momma." She smiled, and Billie Jean stared into her girl's beautiful blue-eyed, pink-lipped face and knew it could be no other than her little Katie.

But how?

As if hearing her thoughts, Katie said, "Momma, this is Heaven! This is my home with Jesus."

Billie Jean's mind began to whirl.

What does it mean? Did I die, and this place, this journey has been part of Heaven?

She stood up quickly, trying not to panic and trying to wrap her mind around the possibilities.

Katie stepped toward her, "Momma?"

Billie Jean stepped back and shook her head and backed into something solid. She slowly turned around and came face to face with the Gryphon again. Everything around her seemed to stop. Suddenly, Katie and the other children were gone, and she was alone with Him. His gemstone eyes pierced her heart with love again. She began to weep.

"Stop! Please! If you love me this much, then why? Why did you take her from me?"Her tears flowed freely now, and she felt the anger and pain of losing her daughter anew.

His gentle voice blew over her soul like a light summer breeze.

Katie was a gift to bring healing to your heart.

"Then why did you take her?" She whispered.

Daughter, I have her, yes, but I did not take her. The enemy, who knows you have a great destiny, sought to derail you from fulfilling what would destroy his works.

She shook her head slowly, "I don't understand."

I give life. There is one in this world who takes life, the Devourer.

"But," She put her hands on her chest. "How am *I* a threat to anyone?"

You don't yet know who you truly are.

She stood silent, thinking about that statement. She definitely didn't know who she was and what her purpose was except to have been a good mother to Katie. Now, she felt purposeless, and any hope for meaning in life had waned to nothing but merely existing.

Billie Jean put her hand over her heart, "Please, I need answers."

The Gryphon stared at her intently with jeweled eyes that radiated the Love of her Savior. It was hard to look away from the strange and beautiful creature, His colorful feathers gleamed as the sunlight reflected off His golden body. The connection to His Spirit was so tangible that His appearance seemed as simple as a colorful hat or dress donned by a close friend.

Watch, Daughter.

Suddenly, she perceived a slight shimmer in the air, followed by a soft breeze with the scent of roses. The trees and grass began to fade, and a classroom slowly appeared.

Billie Jean's eyes widened as she recognized the small room. Bible verses and characters decorated the walls, and eight young children were seated on the familiar, worn blue rug. The kind, young teacher, Ms. Staci, who had made a life-long impact on her as a child, sat in a chair reading a book to the students. Billie Jean quickly scanned the cluster of children and, sure enough, there in front of the teacher were two little girls—one had messy, long, blonde hair and a round face, and the other with neat black hair in two bow-tied pig-tails.

What do you see, daughter?

She heard Him, but when she looked around, she noticed He wasn't physically present with her as she observed the classroom.

"It's me and my best friend, Katie, in Sunday school when we were seven." She said out loud and quickly covered her mouth, worried she disturbed the classroom. But no one turned to look at her, and she visibly relaxed.

Tell me about this day.

She saw Ms. Staci put the book down and speak to the

class, "Who wants to invite Jesus into your heart today?"

Almost all of the children raised their hands—including herself and Katie.

"I remember that day!" Billie Jean's eyes brightened as she smiled. "Katie and her family had been bringing me to church with them. I had gotten to know the kids and teachers and loved it so much! But that day," She pointed to the class. "Ms. Staci asked us if we wanted Jesus...You! in our hearts. I raised my hand and prayed. . ."

What then?

She watched as the little blonde girl closed her eyes, followed the teacher, and prayed. Billie Jean then saw tears slide down the child's face as she bowed her head and clasped her little hands together.

"I . . . felt you change my heart. It was like this heavy, dark blanket lifted off me, and my chest felt warm and safe on the inside. It was like nothing I had ever felt before."

As she watched, there was a shimmer in the air, and the scene faded and changed. She was now standing outside of her childhood home.

Daughter, what do you see?

Billie Jean's heart dropped as she watched herself, now

about eight years old, wearing tattered pink overalls, with ever messy, uncombed hair. Little Billie Jean stared helplessly at her best friend's home across the street as a moving van was being loaded up. Katie and her mom crossed the street, and they both hugged Billie Jean fiercely. Katie handed her a stuffed unicorn, one of her favorites, and Billie Jean clutched the toy close as tears slipped down. Katie and her mom waved goodbye and crossed back over to the truck.

"Oh, that was a hard day when Katie moved." Billie Jean frowned, slowly shaking her head as the feelings began to resurface.

What happened after that day?

"I was alone."

The scene shimmered, and Billie Jean closed her eyes, anticipating the next shift. She took a deep breath and slowly opened her eyes. Crossing her arms and slowly releasing her breath, she looked at the interior of her childhood home. Her eight-year-old self was curled up and crying on the old, stained couch, green with white flowers. She was still holding Katie's stuffed unicorn. After some time, her father walked in the front door with a red-headed woman in a short dress and heels. They were both laughing but stopped abruptly when they saw her.

"Who's she?" the red-head asked with a snarl.

Her father looked annoyed, "*She* is my daughter, Billie Jean, and she'll be excusing herself to her room."

Billie Jean wiped her eyes and quickly got up to leave.

"Hey, what's got you all upset?" he asked as she passed.

Her lip quivered as she looked up at him, "K-Katie moved away today."

"That's tough luck, kid." He patted her shoulder and looked back at his date, smiling. "I'm sure you'll feel better in the morning. Go up to your room now."

A stray tear dropped, she looked down and began to shuffle out, but stopped and turned, "D-dad?"

"What now, kid?!" He briefly looked over at her.

"C-can you take me to church now that I can't go with Katie's family anymore?"

He looked a bit surprised, and he and his date started laughing. After a bit, he looked at Billie Jean with cold eyes and tone, "I'll never step foot in one of those friggin' fake, judgmental, God clubs. Sorry, little girl, you're double outta' luck. Now get to your room!"

She ran up to her room and threw herself on her bed. Feeling completely alone, she cried into her pillow most of the night.

The sight of her younger self's grief made Billie Jean cross her arms tight around herself as if the room was cold. She closed her eyes and rubbed her shoulders and arms, trying to block out the sadness and hurt happening in front of her.

Daughter, I'm here. Open your eyes and look.

She opened her eyes and saw her younger self, still crying into her pillow alone.

"Where, Lord? I don't see you?"

Watch.

Billie Jean watched as the little girl sat up, hiccupping from her tears and putting her hands together to pray, "Jesus, I'm so sad. Please be with me, and please protect Katie and her family when they travel. Amen."

Suddenly, Jesus appeared next to her on the bed with his arms around her, he kissed her head. The younger Billie Jean didn't seem to see him, but the tears stopped, and she lay back down on her pillow and peacefully drifted off to sleep. As she did, Jesus stroked her hair and whispered to her how much He loved her and how she was never alone.

Billie Jean put her hand to her mouth and teared up, "I didn't know you were there with me."

The scene faded, and she was back in her living room. It was dark, except for the TV, which was turned on to some sports channel. Her dad sat on the couch, downing a bottle of beer, a few empty ones scattered all around him.

Slowly, the front door opened, and 17-year-old Billie Jean walked in. She was clad in heels, a black mini-skirt, and a small half-top revealing ample cleavage and the belly of a girl who had begun to carry more voluptuous weight.

In the same instant, she saw him contorted with rage, as he noticed her clothes.

"What in the hell are you wearing!?" He stood up and threw his empty beer bottle on the couch.

She put her hands up in a calming motion, "Daddy, I . . ."

"Don't you *daddy* me, you filthy whore! Where did you just come from dressed like that, walking the streets?!"

"What?! No! I was at a party-" He slapped her, and she fell to the floor from the force, clutching her red face.

"Don't you sass me, you cow! HOW MANY BOYS

HAVE YOU BEEN WITH TONIGHT? Don't think I don't know that you've been whoring around with the other sluts at your school!" He stood over her, red-faced, and pointed down to her as she cowered at the assault of angry words.

Still clutching her face, she shook her head at his accusations. But he pulled her up by her hair as she screamed in pain, and he threw her against the wall, "You can't deny it! Look at you! Showing everything you got, you fat bitch! You think you can live here and come and go as you please!?" He pushed her against the wall again. She quickly moved around him before he could grab her again and ran up to her room as he screamed more profanities after her.

Grown-up Billie Jean looked at the scene, shaking in rage, remembering with fine clarity every word and feeling from that night.

Tell me what you felt that night, Daughter.

Billie Jean wiped a stray tear and thought for a moment, "Rejected. Unwanted. Unloved.

Where were you then, Lord?" She looked around the room, hoping He would appear like he did in the last scene.

I was with you, but you did not call to me like you did before.

"So, why show it to me?"

Billie Jean, invite me into it and let me heal the wound.

She shook her head and put her face in her hands, "What am I supposed to do? Just, like, ask you to heal that memory?"

There was no answer. She looked at the scene again, her father frozen in place at the bottom of the stairs mid-yell. Despite her best efforts at holding in the pain, her tears escaped, slipping down her cheeks as she remembered how much his words had hurt; they were worse than the slap and hair-pulling.

With just a croaking whisper, she asked, "Jesus . . . could you please heal this memory?"

Suddenly, the sweet-smelling breeze blew through again, and Billie Jean realized that she was watching the same memory from the beginning, starting with her dad sitting on the couch drinking.

Her 17-year-old self came in the front door, but as her dad got up to berate her, the scene shifted, and he transformed into Jesus. "Billie Jean, I'm so happy to see you." He embraced her. "You are beautiful!" He released her and looked into her eyes, "I'm so happy that you are my daughter, and I treasure our relationship. Do you know how much I love you, my dear child?"

As He began to speak, Billie Jean went from watching the scene to experiencing it and now stood in her younger self's place in Jesus' arms at the moment He spoke those amazing words to her.

She had no answer to the question he had asked; she shook her head as tears streamed down.

"My sweet princess, you are wanted, completely accepted, and loved by Us more than you could possibly imagine." Amazingly, He also had tear-filled eyes, "We designed every cell, every hair, and every freckle that you have. We excitedly planned your days before any of them existed. We think about you constantly and are always longing for you."

She leaned on his chest and wailed as she allowed His words to heal the deep wound in her soul. He held her for a long time, and when the tears finally began to slow, and she could breathe again, she looked up into His gentle face.

He smiled, "What are you feeling now, Billie Jean?"

She paused, putting her hand on her forehead in wonder. "I feel lighter, my mind is clearer, too. But, oh . . . I'm so spent."

A light breeze stirred the room; she smiled when the lovely rose fragrance blew in with it. The scene faded, and they were back in the colored forest.

"Follow me." Jesus looked at her, His eyes wide with excitement as he jogged away and immediately transformed back into the Gryphon. He spread his amazing colorful wings and took off.

She giggled with excitement as she changed into the white eagle and flew after him, high above the multicolored trees. Billie Jean began to dip and spin above and through vast cotton candy clouds, feeling energy and delight rise in her heart. She kept the beautiful Gryphon in her sights but took her time behind Him to flit and fly with abandon, relishing every moment of glorious flight.

Daughter, who are you? His gentle whisper dropped into her mind.

I don't know, Lord. . . I guess I am who You made me to be.

Who did I create you to be, dear one?

Well . . . I thought Katie's mom. I was good at that.

Yes, you are a good mom, but that isn't who you are. Who are you?

*I am...*she paused, not quite knowing how to answer. *I am who You made me to be. . . I am your daughter.*

Yes, you are most you when you are in union with Me. I in you and you in Me; all connected to Father's heart; complete in Him. As long as you continue to look for your identity outside of Us, you will always be in want.

Gliding on the wind, she let His words cascade through her mind. She turned the words over, struggling to comprehend the full meaning.

Lord, I feel like I've been asleep for a long time, and everything was gray and without meaning. Now I feel like I'm beginning to awaken, and can see the first tinges of tones, and more is coming as You show me.

Yes, my daughter. Come, let me show you something else.

He landed on a desert island with undulating dunes as far as the eye could see. She touched down next to him and transformed into the lion. Although she was a substantial size, she still did not even broach the height of the great Creature's shoulder.

Looking at her intently, he said, "When I first began my earthly ministry, Ruach drove me into the wilderness to be tempted by Satan."

"I remember reading that story and never understood the purpose of it," she answered.

He nodded and continued, "It was manifold, but I didn't yet know fully who I was."

" . . . And the wilderness temptation helped?"

"Now is your time to grasp your identity, daughter. You must go."

"Out there?" She questioned, beginning to get nervous.

"Yes, and without the comfortable outer shells that you've grown to depend on."

Suddenly, she was transformed into her "real world" voluptuous "50 pounds to lose" body replete with her favorite ripped jeans, baggy t-shirt, light zip-up hoodie, and teal low-top Converse sneakers.

Her mouth dropped open, and she began to protest, "But...how...?"

Billie Jean, my daughter...You are never alone.

And with that, He was already in the air and quite a distance away before she believed He really had left her on the desert island.

"Come back!!!" she yelled at the empty sky.

The Waking

You are never alone.

"What am I supposed to do?" she said to the emptiness.

Silence.

"What am I supposed to do?" she said again quietly and pathetically to herself.

There was literally nothing but sand dunes in every direction she looked. Also, based on the heat, this was a *for real* hot and dry desert. Above her, she heard an eagle call and quickly looked up as a golden eagle passed overhead. Her heart skipped, and she ran forward, trying to transform and follow. But she realized she couldn't do that here.

Frustrated, she humphed to herself and began to jog forward, attempting to keep the eagle in her sights. After a little way, she began to huff and puff with exertion and grumble at the state she'd been left in. She quickly lost sight of the eagle over a high dune ahead.

When she got to the dune, she quit jogging, took off her now sweat-drenched hoodie, draped it over her head, and began an extremely slow ascent. Her thoughts drifted to the group, and she wondered what they thought had happened to her. "Probably that the Gryphon ate me." She laughed. "I wish He had just eaten me! This sucks!"

At the top, she got a view of the seemingly perpetual wasteland.

"Screw this!" she yelled to no one in particular. Was she supposed to turn back? "Where am I going to go? This is an effing island!"

Grunting again, she thought she saw movement in the distance. She squinted and saw something black sticking out of the sand, which could've been anything from that range.

Probably a mirage. But it's not like I have better options.

She slowly and clumsily made her way down the other side of the dune and started walking toward the obscure black object.

What seemed like hours later, sweat-drenched and parched, Billie Jean finally found herself within steps of a giant, black, dead tree. The eagle that she had seen earlier was perched on a high up branch, making a disgustingly slow meal out of a snake. She grimaced and proceeded warily toward the base of the great ugly tree. The thick serpentine roots breached the sand in multiple areas for many yards out from the trunk, and Billie Jean had to take care where she stepped to keep from tripping. She began to think the heat was playing tricks on her eyes as the roots seemed to move under the sand as she stepped closer.

Soon, she thought she heard faint screams and weeping coming from the tree. She paused, her breath caught in her throat with fear and worry. Should she run? But what if someone needed her help? What good was she without her powers?

The scream came again, which she was now certain came from the tree itself.

She crouched low, threw her jacket-turban to the side, and crawled carefully and alertly towards the tree. As she reached it, she heard the muffled screams again. She pressed her ear against the trunk and shivered as it felt more like thick, cold reptilian skin than bark, and more weeping and screams confirmed that this was an evil tree in more than just appearance.

"Well, sister dear, you're not going to get much accomplished slinking around. We can certainly see you, so come out! Come around the front end!"

Billie Jean froze, her heart thudding in her ears, so sure before that there was no one nearby. As she still stayed crouched and immobile, two long, pale legs on bare feet strode towards and stopped directly in front of her. She stood up slowly before an incredibly tall, shapely woman with hands on her hips, looking like a testy teacher who has been disobeyed. Billie Jean's 5'10" frame left her at eye view of the lady's ample cleavage pouring out of a skin-tight black leather bodice atop an extremely short skirt. The woman was strikingly beautiful with dark eyes and two long, thick black braids falling behind her.

"And who are you?" the tall woman asked.

Billie Jean, who had no answer to that question, paused. She was no longer afraid but thoughtful.

"Well, speak up, girl! I won't ask *nicely* again!"

Billie Jean dodged the question, "What's inside this tree?"

The woman smirked, "Well, have you come to spy on me then? Who sent you? Yeshua?" Her smirk quickly turned into a snarl, "I'm within my rights here! It's my territory! My domain!"

Another cry came from within the tree. Billie Jean stepped around the woman who grabbed her arm, but Billie Jean spun in the opposite direction, escaping the surprised woman's grip. She dashed around the tree, looking for an opening, adrenaline pumping from fear, and the desire to save the trapped person. Just as Billie Jean found the opening, her foe was upon her attempting to grab her again from behind. She spun out of her grip, and the woman thudded against the tree.

Billie Jean faced her and yelled, "STOP!" with her hand extended in front of her, and amazingly, the woman stopped in her tracks, eyes wide in shock. Billie Jean, also stunned that her command actually worked, stood a moment contemplating her next move.

"I am going in there!" she said sternly to the woman, "And *you* are staying out here!"

The woman looked at her with disdain but nodded a short, reluctant agreement. Billie Jean relaxed a bit, and before she proceeded through the entrance of the tree, she asked the woman, "Who are you?"

The woman answered simply and smugly, "I am Lillith."

Billie Jean shrugged and walked into the tree as another scream rang out. She descended down a dark, winding stairway so small and narrow that she felt a bit dizzy from the continuous turns. After counting 311 stairs from the top, counting helped her stay calm and focused, Billie Jean finally came to a large iron door. When she walked through it into a dungeon filled with cages, she noticed that each cage door was unlocked and cracked open. The prisoners inside-men, women, and children were lying on the floor or huddled in corners, some shaking and crying, some moaning and rocking- weren't trying to escape. She walked by the cells in shock and disbelief. One had a teenage boy squatting fearfully in a corner, and she called out to him, "Hey!" He shrank from her voice.

More gently, she said, "Hey, the door is open, why don't you leave here?" But he just covered his ears and shook his head. She went into the cage and tried to touch him, and he moved away from her in fear.

"Hey, I'm not going to hurt you." She tried to say soothingly. "Please… please listen to me." He continued to move away from her, still holding his hands over his ears. Hearing the cries that initially brought her there, she finally left the boy's cage, sadly shaking her head.

She passed a few more open cages with people inside until she found the one with the screaming woman. This one startled her, and she stepped back as there were two ugly raccoon-sized, humanoid goblins tormenting the pris-oner. She watched as a blonde woman cowered in a corner, head down as the monsters stood near her, shouting insults, "No one wants you! Your mother didn't want you! Your father didn't want you! You're weak! You're worthless! No one sees you! No one cares about you!" The young woman nodded each time they threw a new insult at her, weeping and crying but in complete agreement with the monsters. "You're fat! Unlovable! You're trash!"

Billie Jean got angrier and angrier as the ugly creatures danced with glee, tearing this poor woman apart. She seemed unable to move or defend herself even though she, too, was in an unlocked cage. Finally, Billie Jean had had enough, and she burst into the cage. The startled creatures squealed in fright. She made quick work of them, kicking one hard as if it were a soccer ball, sending it flying against the cage wall. The other shrieked and scampered out, but not before getting a kick in the backside, helping it along.

Billie Jean quickly went to the prisoner and knelt next to her, "Are you okay?"

The crying woman slowly looked up, moving her long blonde hair out of her face. Billie Jean sprang back against the cage wall, mortified to see her own tear-stained face staring back up at her.

"Oh, my God! What is happening!?" Billie Jean took a tentative step back towards the lady, staring intently at her face. After rubbing her eyes a couple times, and still seeing it was her own face, she began to pace and take deep breaths.

The woman looked at her, puzzled, "Who are you?"

"Why do people keep asking me that?!" Billie Jean threw her arms up in frustration.

The other Billie Jean clamped her mouth shut, looking hurt.

Billie Jean sighed and ran her hands through her mop of hair, "I'm sorry. I didn't mean to snap at you, okay?" The woman relaxed a bit and nodded.

She pulled the woman to her feet and looked "herself" in the eye. The hopelessness looking back at her broke Billie Jean's heart. Could this really be her? She moved a strand of hair out of the poor woman's face, "Who are you? Why do you look like me? How did you get in here?"

Her other self was wide-eyed, "I ...I ...I'm Unwanted...I'm Unloved. I ...I don't know. I think I've always been here."

"What? What are you saying?" She looked into "her" eyes again, and something clicked.

Was this sad shell her true self?

Who are you?

She heard His voice again.

Save her. Tell her who she truly is.

"Look at me." Billie Jean held her by the shoulders and looked into 'her' sad blue eyes. Her heart ached to reach the woman.

"All that you heard from those—things...were lies! You are wanted! You are loved! Your name is Billie Jean, and you are the daughter of the King of the Universe! He loves you! He chose you! You are a great warrior and capable of amazing things!" She began to smile as she told herself these truths. "You are a hero and are going to save the world! And the freaking Devil is afraid of you!"

As she spoke, she could see life coming back into the eyes of her other self. *She* was starting to believe her.

Billie Jean paused for a moment, tearing up, "I'm so sorry that I ever agreed with the enemy that you . . . that *I* was not worthy of love."

When she said that, the tear-streaked woman hugged her tightly. Billie Jean really loved this woman and realized how much she had mistreated her over the years. She whispered to her, "I promise, I won't treat you like that anymore."

While they embraced, the blonde woman suddenly disappeared. Billie Jean felt the woman become a part of her again, as if a piece of her heart, once broken off, was put perfectly back into place. She also felt something like a filling up happen in her belly, and she laughed out loud.

Suddenly, the cage and dungeon disappeared, and Billie Jean was back in the colored forest with the Gryphon. Incredible joy overtook her, and she couldn't stop laughing. She laughed with her whole body until tears poured down her cheeks. Sitting down, she began to fully experience every sweet flowery smell, every clear thought, the feel of the soft grass beneath her, and the familiar giggles from somewhere close by. She turned her head, and Katie tackled her with a big hug. They both giggled, and a tickle war ensued.

"You look so happy, Momma!" Katie put her hand on Billie Jean's face again.

"I am happy, baby. Happier than I've been in a long, long time."

CHAPTER 9

The day slowly faded into twilight, and the warriors finally made it to the top of Mount Joy. They navigated through a cluster of trees that eventually opened into a flat clearing. The area was wide enough to hold a large number of people, and at the center of the clearing, three men tended a fire.

Diego and the team approached the strangers cautiously. One of them casually turned to them as if he had been waiting for them to arrive, "Come weary ones, join us at the fire. Eat, drink, and rest. Do not be afraid."

The one who had spoken approached. With a kind smile, the man grasped Diego's hand firmly, "Come, Diego, eat!"

Diego visibly relaxed and turned to the others, "Come young ones, the Lord has provided for us."

The group gathered around the fire, grateful to warm themselves and have a place to rest after the earlier battle and long trek. The trio of bearded, dark-skinned men were dressed in simple clothing and cloaks, and welcomed them with warm smiles, encouraging the warriors to join them for a meal. The smell of roasting meat from the fire instantly captured their weary attention, and the kind strangers began handing out plate after plate of food, loaves of hot bread, and cups of sweet wine.

The men talked very little at first, letting the group eat and drink their fill without pressure. Once the weary warriors had eaten their fill, they began to relax a bit and talk of the day while the men listened intently and asked questions. Darrel watched them closely, silent and skeptical of the free hospitality.

"Why do you doubt us, Darrel?" inquired the man who had first invited them over.

Darrel was surprised he said his name but refused to show it. "Doubt? I don't know what you're talking about, man."

"Ah, but you do doubt! You don't know how to take us. Strangers offering food and rest… for free?" The man looked Darrel in the eye, "But I do know you, Darrel James Coleman." As he said Darrel's full name, the man's eyes glowed briefly. In response, Darrel's heart quickened and burned; he looked down.

The man's voice dropped gently into Darrel's thoughts.

Darrel, I know you. I've always known you. Even when

you tried to run from me and ignore me, I have never left you.

Darrel began shaking as he realized that he was in the presence of the Lord. He slowly looked up at the man, tears in his eyes. "But *I* left *You*. I broke my word to You. What do You want with me, Lord?"

The man stood up and said, "Follow me." He then walked away from the fire toward the trees. Darrel looked at the others, who were still eating and wrapped in conversation with the other two strangers. He quickly got up and followed the man into the wooded area. They strode away from the fire, the half-moon rising high above them, cast just enough light to see their steps. The man said nothing else until he stopped outside a cave entrance.

He leaned against the outside wall and looked intently at Darrel.

"You must go in—alone."

"What's in there?"

"Only what you take with you."

Darrel examined the face of the familiar stranger, whose remarkable kind eyes were bright and visible even though all else was in shadow. The man didn't offer any more instruction, so Darrel nodded to him, cracked his neck, and stepped into the dark cave. Again, he was thankful for his particular gift in this strange world, where he constantly walked through dark places. He opened his hand and produced a flame, illuminating the cave.

There was one way to go, and that was forward into darkness. He walked steadily for quite a while on a path that seemed to slope downward. After some time, he began to get nervous that he would be stuck in this dark cave until he died. He decided to steer his thoughts away from death and forced them to focus on the man he left at the cave entrance. Was it really Him? Jesus? He was sure of it at the fire but now began to have his doubts.

This whole journey was crazy, and he still expected to wake up at any time… but it felt real enough, especially after getting scratched, bit, and beat in the earlier battle with Satan's winged girlfriends. He shook his head and chuckled to himself, promptly sending a loud echo throughout the quiet cave tunnel.

Thinking about the harpies brought Billie Jean back to mind. He had just met her a couple of days ago but really liked her. She was gorgeous, yes, but sweet and mysterious too. She talked just enough to make him want to know more, and he really hoped she would come back soon.

Suddenly, the sound of water ahead broke him out of his thoughts. He quickened his pace and soon came into a vast, open area with a large pool of water in the center, which flowed to what sounded like a waterfall far behind. With light coming out of the pool, Darrel extinguished his flame. The area around the pool was surrounded by glowing, water-filled doorways. Each doorway also radiated a different color, but he couldn't see what was beyond them. Curious, he approached a green-blue one, and as he got closer, realized he could see his own reflection in the water-filled entrance. Impossibly, the water didn't spill out, but stayed at the threshold, as if it were a pool in the ground.

What am I, in Wonderland?

He nervously chuckled at the thought.

Cautiously, he put one finger in, and his reflection mirrored the action. He felt the cool, wet water and nothing else out of the ordinary, so he continued to put his whole hand through. As his hand went in, he was amazed that it felt dry as it passed the water's surface. He quickly pulled it out and, sure enough, found no dampness.

"What the-?"

He stood there for a moment, struggling to make sense of the weirdness. He put his hands on his hips and wrestled the conflicting ideas of *go with the flow* versus *run from the crazy*. Finally, the irrational side prevailed. "Well, I'm here," he shrugged to himself, "Let's go and get this done."

Darrel closed his eyes and walked into the water. It was a strange sensation of cold and wet, then dry and warm again. Suddenly, he had arrived at his office and saw himself sitting behind the desk with his most notorious client seated in front of him: Peter "Primo" Williams.

He rubbed his eyes and shook his head, but nothing changed, and he was still standing there watching a memory like he was Scrooge, only there was no ghost helping him navigate the wackiness.

"Primo" was affiliated with the Bloods and the Sex Money Murder gangs in the Bronx. He had carved out an empire by flooding the streets with cocaine, opioids, and his tentacles could also be tied into sex trafficking and gun-running. Darrel and Petey had been childhood friends, the reason why he approached Darrel to defend him when he had his most recent run-in with the law.

"Petey, why are you coming to me? There's plenty of

big-time defense attorneys out there who would be willing to take your case."

"My brother, D," His grin shined with a gold and diamond grill that Darrel imagined cost more than his Mercedes. "I don't know any of those other lawyers...I want to give you the chance to take my case and make you famous." If you win this case for me, D, I can make all of your wildest dreams come true. Money, fame, you name it. I have the power to make it happen."

In the memory, Darrel was silent, keeping his poker face perfectly. Meanwhile, the wheels of his mind spun with intensely conflicting thoughts.

The Darrel, who was observing, was shaking his head. This was it, the crossroads. This was the moment where he really went to the devil. He hated reliving this memory, and it brought heavy guilt and shame.

Darrel knew that the pause he took, which wasn't long enough, was his battle with the voice. That Voice in his heart told him, even in past choices, he was heading down the wrong road. That each small wrong choice led to another, becoming a slippery slope of terrible decisions that he couldn't turn back from.

At the desk, Darrel asked, "What if I can't win in

court? The evidence against you is pretty solid."

Peter reeked of arrogance, his ebony-colored eyes reminding Darrel of a snake. Again, he smiled wide, "Darrel, I have people who can help with that; there's no way we can lose. I just need you to say yes, my friend."

Darrel stood up quickly, reaching his hand out, "Okay, Petey. I'll take your case."

Likewise, Peter stood up, shaking Darrel's hand and giving him a brief hug, "You won't regret it, my friend."

The office disappeared, and Darrel was outside the blue cave entrance staring at his reflection once again. He growled and struck at the water, only succeeding in splashing himself in the face, so he turned from it with a frustrated grunt. He did not want to do this, he did not want to be here thinking about the mess that he made of things by saying yes to that piece of garbage, Peter Williams.

It's true if he could go back and change that day, he would. The money and prestige were bittersweet. He had tried to enjoy it, but he knew he had sold his soul when he "won" the case—if you can call it winning to pay off police to lose evidence and jury members to lie. To forget his shame, Darrel enjoyed the money by taking nice trips with beautiful women, buying a couple of cars, and gifting his grandma elegant clothing and furniture. But every time he went to visit her, he saw the gangs and dealers on the streets and knew inside he was just like them.

He hated himself. But he hid it behind a smug demeanor, false grin, and beautiful suits. He had learned to ignore the feelings by working more and being alone less. He quickly climbed the ladder of success as his work ethic and notoriety kept clients constantly streaming through his office door.

Darrel yelled out to the cavern, "I did the best I could with what I had! What do you want from me?!"

His own echo was the only response. He rubbed his head and frowned. After watching Lincoln and Gianna's life and weaknesses displayed for all to see, he had deliberately steered clear of sharing any of his true self with the individuals he had met here. His doubt and fear had caused him to turn inward to avoid the confrontation with his past that he felt was coming. Now, he realized there was no way to evade his past. His stomach clenched, and he wished for a way of escape, but he also knew the fastest way out of a tough situation is to simply plow ahead like a warrior. What choice did he have?

He stepped to the next doorway, glowing red. He glared

at his reflection and stepped through, but he couldn't see well because of the dazzling brightness on the other side. It took his eyes a minute to adjust, and when they did, he was looking at a very tall, handsome man in a black suit with slicked-back black hair and cold, coal-black eyes.

Pointing at him, the man said, "This is the one, Your Honor. He's guilty of treason against this court, and therefore, I move that all his gifts and blessings that You have given him, be stripped immediately!"

Darrel's heart began to beat wildly as he tried to grasp who this man was and where he had stepped into. Then another voice spoke, from before a humongous throne, "Your Honor, I object, Darrel Coleman belongs to me. I paid for him already with my own blood, let Me prove he's still worthy of Your call and blessings."

A voice boomed from the throne and shook the whole room as He spoke, "State your cases."

Darrel tried to look up at the Great Being sitting on the throne, but He was too glorious, and Darrel quickly looked away. A majestic angel dressed in white came to the center of what he could now clearly see was a courtroom. "The Almighty Ancient of Days will now hear the accusation against Darrel James Coleman brought by The Satan. Darrel Coleman, please approach the throne."

Darrel took a deep breath and walked forward, and as he did, his clothing changed from the flaming wrestling pants to a pure white suit with a white shirt and tie, along with white shoes tipped in gold. He instantly felt in his element.

Adjusting his tie, Darrel looked at his accuser, who apparently was the Prince of Darkness himself. Darrel sized him up quickly. He was the most good-looking white man he had ever seen: tall, well-built, and very sure of himself as he smirked mockingly in Darrel's direction. Then he looked at the Man who had defended him. The Son of God, also dressed in white, wore regal robes laced with gold instead of a suit. He had the same kind face as the man by the fire earlier, but now, He was undeniably kingly and majestic. He looked at Darrel tenderly as he walked up, and the stoic angel asked, "Darrel Coleman, how do you plead?"

Darrel stood up straight and tilted his head toward the Being on the throne and, without much thought, stated, "Not guilty, Your Honor."

The Great Voice shook the courtroom again, "Present your case, Accuser."

Lucifer smiled smugly, "Thank you, Your Honor. The Prosecution calls Darrel J. Coleman to the witness stand."

Suddenly, Darrel was seated in a witness box, and Satan was staring at him with his piercing black eyes.

"Mr. Coleman. Please state your name, age, and what you do for a living."

Darrel quickly turned off any visible facial expression and turned on his 'business' face. "Darrel James Coleman, age 32. I'm a defense attorney."

"Would you say," Satan paused a beat. "that you are successful?"

Darrel, almost instinctively, adjusted his tie again. "Yes, I'm one of the top three in my office for cases won. I'm currently being considered as a partner for the firm, and I make great money."

"Did you grow up well off and privileged?"

"No, quite the opposite, actually. I never knew my father, and my mother was a drug addict. So, I was raised by my grandmother and didn't have much growing up."

"When you say you didn't have much, do you mean you went hungry?" The Accuser casually put his hands in his suit pockets. "Please . . . Describe your home life for us."

He paused for a moment, wondering how much was necessary to share with the Devil, of all people. But God Himself knew everything already, so Darrel decided that there was no point in editing.

He began thoughtfully, "No, grandma always made sure there was food on the table and clothes on my back. We didn't go out much, and I didn't wear name brands or have a lot of extravagant things. But it was enough. The neighborhood was rough, a lot of gangs and drugs, and the schools lacked a lot of resources. I never felt unsafe, though, I just knew where to go and not to go to stay out of trouble. Plus, my grandma kept me in church, where there were a lot of activities and great mentors for the kids involved. It really kept my head on straight."

He ran his hand across his bald head.

". . . but I saw and experienced my share of hard things. My mom was in and out of jail. I had friends who joined gangs, got shot, and went to jail. My grandma really kept me grounded and told me I could do anything if I followed Jesus and made good choices. I followed her advice."

"Oh, how sad. I'm sure that was difficult for you growing up," Satan tssked, grasped his hands casually behind his back, and smiled. "But was following your grandma's advice truly what led you out of that harsh environment and into favor and success?"

"Well, yes and no." Darrel cleared his throat and squirmed a bit for the first time since donning the sleek suit. "I was really involved in youth group and community service activities. I also did really well in school. During my senior year in high school, I got nominated for an academic scholarship to a prestigious university. There was a lot of competition for this scholarship—more than 1,000 people. I wrote the essay, filled out the application, sent it in, and prayed. Truthfully, I didn't think I had much of a chance. But I was chosen, and the rest was history."

Satan smirked, "Oh, sounds like you got a brush of good luck!" He raised his eyebrows, "But, was that all? Have you really told us the whole story, Mr. Coleman?"

Darrel adjusted his tie again, "Of course, there was more… I mean, yes, I prayed for God's help, and He answered."

The Accuser tssked again and shook his head, "Now, now, Mr. Coleman." Satan got uncomfortably close to Darrel's face. "You are in the heavenly court, are you really going to testify here," he gestured to the court. ". . . that it was *merely* an answered prayer?"

Darrel shifted away from the Devil's face, "I don't know what you mean."

Lucifer turned quickly to the Judge, "Your Honor, may I present evidence to the court?"

"Proceed." The Voice boomed from the throne.

The courtroom disappeared in a whirlwind, and Darrel was suddenly standing in his grandmother's kitchen, watching her and his 10-year-old self, sitting at the small table. His younger self was in tears with an uneaten piece of apple pie sitting in front of him.

"Honey, your mama won't be gone for long. Only a couple of months in jail then a month in the rehab center, and she'll be back for you. It will be just fine; Grandma will take good care of you."

He ran his sleeve across his runny nose and tried to talk through his tears, "Wha, what abo- about ma-my dad?"

"Baby, you haven't seen that man in months," She put her hands on her hips, "Do you think he's going to be able to take care of you? We'll be lucky to get a phone call, let alone any care or money for it."

He began to cry more. His grandma came around the table, turned his chair towards her, and bent down, "Listen,

Honey. I know it's hard right now, but I'm gonna' do my best to make sure you're taken care of. The Bible says, even if my father and mother forsake me, the Lord will hold me close. God is our good Father, no matter what kind of parents we have on this earth, you hear me?" Little Darrel nodded, and big Darrel wiped away the stray tears the memory provoked.

The kitchen disappeared, and Darrel was at his childhood church that his grandma took him to. There, he watched his 16-year-old self sitting with the youth pastor, Craig.

"Darrel, I'm glad you came early today. I wanted to talk to you."

"Oh yeah? What about?"

Craig smiled, "I've noticed how you've been volunteering for every community outreach and youth fundraising activity the last few months, Darrel. You've really stepped up to go the extra mile with giving your time and effort. The other kids notice too and have been volunteering more just to do what you're doing. I wanted to see if you would be interested in taking more of a formal leadership role in the youth ministry once you turn 17."

The scene changed again, and 17-year-old Darrel was

filling out forms for an academic scholarship to Columbia University. He wrote what he thought was one of the best essays he'd ever read, but he knew his chances were slim.

Pastor Craig had been telling him to pray and see how the Lord would come through for him. Darrel had his doubts. Why would God do this for him? He was no one special. He wasn't even sure he fully believed in all this church stuff. It made his grandma happy that he was in church, and he liked the youth group, and he definitely liked all the attention he got once he was in leadership. So, would God really help him? It couldn't hurt to ask.

Darrel bowed his head over his paper and prayed, "God, I know I don't pray a lot. I don't even know if you are really even hearing me right now. But I really want to get out of this neighborhood and do something with my life. I know if I got a chance, then I could be great! If you help me get that scholarship to Columbia, I promise I'll work hard and become a great lawyer. If I do that, I'll serve you with my whole heart, and I'll help people. I'll help people who get taken advantage of and the poor who can't afford a lawyer. Just let me get the chance, God, please. Just give me the chance. Amen."

Darrel got ready for bed and laid down. And as soon as

his head hit the pillow, he heard a voice.

"Darrel, my son, I've heard your prayer, and I accept your terms. I am granting your request."

Darrel sat up in bed, his heart racing, "Hello?! God?" only silence came. He listened for a long time, but the Voice didn't come again, and Darrel finally fell asleep.

The scene faded, and suddenly Darrel watched as he graduated from Columbia Law school a few years later. He walked across the stage with honors, and his grandma, other family members, and church friends came to celebrate. Even though many he loved and cared about came, a bitter dart entered his heart when he saw who hadn't shown. After the ceremony, Darrel went to hug his grandma. He looked around her.

"Grandma, where is my mom? I thought you said she was coming?"

His grandma shook her head sadly.

"Oh, baby, I'm sorry. She didn't show up when we were all leaving to come here. I'm sure she would've come if she could."

Darrel looked angry and hurt but shook it off. "That's

alright. She hasn't been there my whole life; can't expect she would show up now either."

Darrel couldn't help but feel the sting again as he watched his younger self put on a mask of toughness when inside he hurt so badly. He sighed, grinding his teeth in an effort to, yet again, hold back the emotions that clawed the thin walls of his resolve. He turned from the scene as it changed back to the heavenly courtroom. He was again seated in the witness box facing Satan.

"Mr. Coleman, that must have been hard to watch. Did that last part stir up some negative emotion?" the Accuser chided with a grin.

Darrel was silent. Satan turned back to The Judge smugly.

"Your Honor, we're all witness to the vow he made when he prayed to you at 17 years old. He said he would defend the poor and disenfranchised if you helped him get into that school and become a lawyer! You clearly fulfilled *your* word to him, but what did he do in the seven years he's had his law license? We all know the answer to this, right?"

Satan gestured widely to the whole courtroom where angels and saints were standing witness. There was silence from all. Darrel's stomach churned, and he dropped his head, knowing what was coming. Guilt and shame blanketed him as he knew his culpability was apparent to the whole Universe.

Satan continued, "He rose to fame and prosperity by defending drug dealers and crime bosses! The very ones perpetuating drugs, crime, and terror in the neighborhood he grew up in! Defender of the poor? Ha! He traded integrity for money! Is there any doubt?"

Darrel could no longer hold back the torrent as unbidden tears began running down his face. He knew there was no escaping the truth. He had helped some of the worst scum of society escape justice on technicalities. Even though he had no respect for gang leaders and drug runners like Peter Williams, they made it well worth his while to defend them, paying triple what anyone else paid for a good defense. He definitely enjoyed spending the money he had received. How many times had he pushed the Voice away in his heart that urged him to repent and take a different path? The one that reminded him no amount of money was worth what he was a party to? He knew he deserved punishment for helping those monsters continue their lives of crime at the expense of the poor. He had broken his vow to God and betrayed his own people.

"Look! He knows he's guilty! Mr. Coleman, how do you plead now that you can't hide from the evidence?!" Lucifer practically shouted.

Darrel stood up, shaking, "Your Honor, I admit it. I broke my word to You, and I have done nothing but selfishly use the gift you gave me for my own pleasure and gain, and I- I deserve whatever punishment you see fit to give me. . . but, Your Honor, I may not deserve it, but I ask for another chance—another chance to do right. I have it in me to make better choices, and I want to . . . I want to help people."

Lucifer smiled smugly, "Your Honor, this man doesn't deserve to keep what you have given him; all the evidence shows this. I implore the court to remove Your blessings and protection from him today!"

The Great Voice spoke, "We will now hear the defense."

Lucifer's smile instantly disappeared, but he moved to the side to allow the opposition to have His say.

The Son of Man stepped forward, His brightness made Darrel drop his head again.

His voice was both powerful and comforting. "Father, Darrel became mine, as a child, by faith and through the confession of his own mouth. Yes, he has sinned and broken his vow. But did he not just confess his sin? Then we are faithful and just to forgive him and cleanse him from all unrighteousness. The Blood is still in effect."

A rumble moved through the room like a mild earthquake.

"He's destined to do great exploits for Us, and he's asked for another chance. His road will be hard, but I believe he will trust Us to help him do what he has been called to do."

Satan shrieked in protest, his voice shrill and oily compared to the Son of Man's. "No! No! He still has sin in his heart. Greed! Apathy! Unforgiveness! Lust! He is unacceptable!"

Darrel heard each word of the Accuser, and like daggers, they penetrated his heart. He wept and nodded in agreement with Satan. He was a dirty sinner; he was slime. How could the Good Savior stand in defense of *him?*

The witness stand disappeared, and he crumpled in a fetal position on the courtroom's marble floor, his heart broken with the pain of his guilt. Suddenly, he felt Jesus take him in his arms and cradled him like a child. Darrel struggled to comprehend it, but he was a child in the

Savior's arms. As a child, he could look at His brightness without fear.

Jesus lovingly wiped Darrel's tears away, "My son, you are forgiven. All the sins that have enslaved you are washed away, and the chains broken off of you."

Jesus then stood child-Darrel on his feet and knelt in front of him. Darrel stared into His kind eyes and felt a weight of guilt and shame lift off of his shoulders.

"Look, I'm giving you a new heart, and I'm putting a new spirit in you." With that, the Savior took his own heart out, a bright sphere of pulsing red light, and put it into Darrel's chest. The powerful exchange sent bolts of energy and light between them. Darrel took a deep breath and instantly felt life, love, peace, and joy run through his body. He reached up and hugged Jesus.

"Thank you! Thank you!"

As they stepped out of the embrace, Darrel was his adult self again, standing before the Judge of the Universe, who boomed, "The Court rules in favor of the accused!"

The laugh of joy from the Creator shook the whole court like an earthquake. The angels and saints then erupted in screams and applause. Darrel couldn't stop smiling as he looked around the bright and joyous room.

The only sour face in the courtroom was Lucifer, who was seething in rage. He glared at Darrel, then disappeared in a puff of dark, oily smoke. Darrel shivered from the cold evil that had come off him. Jesus slapped Darrel on the back, grinning widely.

"Don't give him a thought, son. Come on, it's time to re-join your team. There's so much more!"

Darrel raised his eyebrows questioningly. A portal opened, and Jesus gestured for them to walk through. The two arrived back inside the cave with the colored pool and doorways.

Darrel noticed that he was back in his flaming wrestling pants, and Jesus was, again, the inconspicuous traveler. They walked out of the cave in silence, Darrel pondering deeply all that had just taken place. After a bit, Darrel turned to Jesus, "Master?"

"I'm here, my son."

"I'm going to do better." He looked down, absently moving dirt around with his boot.

"When I get back, I'm going to give away all the money I got from defending criminals. I'm going to quit my firm and start my own, and I'll defend people who are disenfranchised and mistreated. I'll fulfill my vow."

Jesus hugged Darrel tight, "I know you will, my son." He pulled back and looked at him, "I have even bigger plans than that for you, though. Wait and see."

Darrel again raised his eyebrows.

"Come. They're waiting for us."

When they got closer to the clearing to join the others, he heard a voice he didn't expect and quickened his pace. As he came upon the group sitting around the fire, he couldn't contain his happiness. There she was, in her beautiful human form, sitting with the others talking away about her adventure: Billie Jean.

She stopped talking when he arrived and smiled up at him.

CHAPTER 10

Darrel and Billie Jean took turns relating their recent adventures, which elicited many tears from everyone. It was evident, in his more relaxed demeanor, that Darrel was a changed man. The walls of arrogance had come down, and for the first time, he let people truly get a glimpse of who he was. He astounded everyone as he related facing Satan in the heavenly courts. Diego peppered him with questions about the angels and the Father, wanting detailed descriptions of it all, which Darrel eagerly gave. Gianna, for one, noticed his ease with everyone as he spoke, where before he had seemed reluctant, making it apparent that, given another option, he would have chosen to talk to anyone else.

Billie Jean, who was also enthusiastically answering questions, had likewise changed. Gianna noted that Billie Jean's beauty seemed enhanced with her new freedom and that Gianna no longer felt jealous. Billie Jean had dropped the protective, arms-length aloofness and really seemed to open up as she shared. Her eyes appeared clearer, the slouch of her shoulders was gone, and her smile more genuine. Darrel, along with everyone else, hung on every word she uttered. And Gianna and Lucy were both moved to tears by the Father's loving heart for Billie Jean.

Yeshua, the Lord, whom they all now understood was their new friend at the fire, listened as intently as the others, and laughed and cried with them at their joy and pain. Darrel revealed Him when he told his story. They were stunned but quickly realized their hearts already knew, as they had suddenly noticed a burning that wasn't there before. Gianna, longing to connect with Him again, continued to glance at Him while the others talked. He was dressed so humbly and was so similar to the other two strangers, whom she assumed were angels, that one would never know there was a difference in rank or status. Yet, here was The King of the Universe sitting amongst them by the fire. She was overcome and had to concentrate to keep from weeping at the knowledge of His close physical proximity. As if sensing her thoughts, He smiled warmly at her. His words drifted into her mind.

Peace, Daughter. You have My heart.

A tear escaped her eye as her heart responded. *Master, I need You desperately.*

You see Me now, but I'm always with you. I've never left you. Not one second.

She didn't answer with words but turned back to

Billie Jean, who was still talking. When she finished, Jesus stepped forward and addressed them all.

"You have all done so well and come so far, dear ones. I had no doubt that each one of you would succeed in this part of your journey. . ." He paused and looked at each of them, intently. The crackling fire threw light and shadow on the dewy-eyed company gathered around it. They looked up at their Savior, hanging on His words with quiet anticipation.

The Lord's companions stood cross-armed and attentive behind Jesus as He continued, "I'm equally certain that this next, difficult and crucial part will be just as victorious. The enemy knows his time is short, and he's angry. He hates you and all of humanity, and he wants to destroy as many as he can before his judgment. Even now, he and his princes are working on a plan for the complete destruction of all flesh. I am sending you, my children, to stop him."

They were stunned. Gianna and Lucy looked at each other, nervously. Darrel, having just come from a victory against Lucifer himself, just smiled, confident of their ability to win with Jesus on their side. Diego nodded. This information confirmed some of what the Holy Spirit had spoken about to him before the journey began.

"During the generations of my beloved servant, Enoch, a faction of 200 angelic beings called Watchers met on the top of Mount Hermon, near present-day Israel. In that meeting, the rebel princes formulated a plan to corrupt humanity and creation to the point of the complete eradication of pure human DNA. Partly because they hated that We created our children in Our image and partly because they wished to stop Our plan of salvation through the seed of the woman. Messiah, the anointed one, had to be born of human seed to fulfill the righteous requirements of the law. The enemy believed that tainting all human bloodlines with fallen angelic DNA...would prevent me from ever coming to fulfill the prophecy."

A cool breeze picked up, and one of the Lord's companions added more wood to the fire. Billie Jean, who was leaning on Darrel, moved a bit closer to it.

Jesus sat down to enjoy a bit more warmth as well, and they waited for Him to continue, "This coupling of the human and angelic DNA resulted in monstrous and violent hybrid creatures called Nephilim. They were also known as giants, titans, and demi-gods. The Fallen ones didn't stop at corrupting only human seed, they also violated animals, resulting in horrendous offspring including centaurs, minotaurs, satyrs, and much more."

Gianna's mind whirled as she took in what He was saying. Her bookworm mind paged through the many fantasy and mythology tales that she'd devoured in her lifetime, and she wrestled with the possibilities of them containing truth. *Real myths?*

"Wait. Wait. Wait...that's real? Not just *this* weird-world real, but like actually in our world too?" Lucy asked with wide eyes. "Giants and centaurs? Like in Greek Mythology that we learned in school?"

Diego stroked his beard, "That makes sense, yes, that the truth was hidden in mythology, and yet I remember that Genesis, chapter six, clearly states that the Sons of God lay with human women and produced giant progeny. I believe the verse called them gibborim 'men of renown.' It has always fascinated me, that chapter."

Jesus nodded. "You are correct, Diego, there is much truth hidden in myth, and much hidden in plain sight. The Scriptures also speak of individuals being anointed to slay those 'mighty men.' Joshua, David and his warriors, as well as Abraham and Noah, were all some of these giant slayers. I don't want any of you to fear, though you will see horrible things. I am anointing a new generation of giant slayers, and you six are the first of many."

Many in the group were nervous and shocked by these new revelations.

Jesus clapped and rubbed his hands together, excitedly, "Yes, it's shocking and awesome! The enemy has his plans, but he will not succeed."

"I don't mean any disrespect, Lord," interjected Darrel, "But you're God. Why not just wipe that guy and all his plans out yourself? Why do you even need us?"

Gianna nodded in agreement with Darrel.

Yeah, she thought. *They were amateurs. God should wipe them out Himself. Why take a chance with unseasoned warriors?*

"Good questions Darrel and Gianna . . ."

"Gianna didn't say anything," Lucy raised her eyebrows.

"Yes, I did," Gianna stammered "…in my mind.."

Jesus continued without acknowledging their surprise, "Why use unseasoned warriors instead of well-trained black-ops types or even wipe them out Ourselves?" Jesus looked around at each of them. "Well, firstly, the enemy underestimates my people constantly, and he needs to see that his time is short, and he will be thwarted in his schemes by my children." He stood, resting his hand on Lincoln's shoulder. "Secondly, my sons and daughters do not understand who they are and what they are capable of. You, my children, can do so much more than you think you can, especially now that you have come through all that you have these last few days."

He stopped speaking. The wind picked up, and the fire danced, causing His eyes to flicker like the flames. Each of them heard His voice drift into their hearts as they sat still, unable to break from His gaze.

Adonai is with you, Oh Mighty Warrior!

Then they heard an answering voice boom across the mountain, "Yes, I am! And I will glorify My Name through my chosen vessels!"

They gasped.

"The voice you heard was to help you believe," He said gently. "Now, stand up! Follow me," he proceeded to offer each lady a hand up.

"Where are we going?" asked Lucy.

He gave her a quick hug, "Come and see."

They all, including the Lord's two companions, quickly followed behind him, curiosity and excitement mixed with a slight uneasiness filled their bellies. Darrel noticed they were heading back towards the cave he had come out of earlier and wondered if they would see the heavenly court again.

Yeshua stopped at the entrance to the cave and turned, "No, Darrel we are not going to the heavenly courtroom at this time,"

Darrel shook his head and grinned, "That is too much with the mind reading, Lord."

He slapped Darrel on the shoulder and chuckled, "Darrel! Wait and see what wonders come next! Okay, everyone follow me, and I'll explain more when we get inside."

They stood at the edge of a large pool in an enormous cavern, which boasted various sized stalactites and stalagmites. A waterfall sounded in the distance. Colored light came from the water-filled doorways that encircled the area, each a unique and distinct hue from the others. Darrel had been here before, but now that it was day, he could take in a lot more detail. The light from above, along with the doorways, threw colored ripples on the cave walls and columns, giving the impression of life and movement. Each of the warriors rotated in wide-eyed fascination, slowly taking in the sights of the cave.

After a short pause, Jesus gestured like a teacher calling to his class, "Gather round, my young warriors."

Jesus stood by the water's edge, which lightly lapped at their feet. Diego chuckled to himself as he walked up with the group. "Young warrior."

Jesus embraced him and remarked, "Diego, *all* are my children, and *all* are young no matter what age!" He grinned. "What is 60 years to a Being who is Infinite?"

Thoughtful, Diego nodded, "You are right, Lord. I'm so used to my current life-role that it is sometimes difficult for me to see myself as a child."

"Son," Jesus looked Diego in the eyes, and his hands on Diego's shoulders, "I'm still counting on you to lead and guide this team; however, you must break the mindsets that have kept you bound up in doubt and fear over the years. It is not weakness to lean into me as a child does with his mother, nor is it weak to cry on my lap as I hold you and pour my love into you. I long for you to allow me to take the heavy burdens from your shoulders."

Diego, overwhelmed by His Master's love, looked down. He clenched his teeth, trying to hold back the tide of emotion even as his body shook from the sobs beginning to erupt from his belly. As he leaned on the Savior's chest, Jesus whispered into his ear, "Let go, Diego."

He held him as he wailed, releasing years of pent up emotions that he had never allowed himself to express. He didn't realize, until then, that he could cry and let go of what he had always seen as weakness. He was supposed to be the strong one, the one who comforted and protected those he loved. The more he cried, the better he felt, so he wept until no more tears came. He pulled back and looked at Jesus, who wiped the stray tears from his cheeks.

"Oh my! Diego, how do you feel?" Jesus remarked with a kind smile.

Diego took a deep breath, "I feel so light and refreshed, like a thousand pounds have been lifted from my shoulders! And such joy!"

They hugged each other again, and suddenly many arms were around them; the whole group had joined the hug. They immediately felt the joy of the Lord fall on them like a blanket, which caused an eruption of laughter, tears, and more hugging from everyone—including the two angels who hadn't shown much emotion up until that moment.

CHAPTER 11

Yeshua addressed them again, "It's time you formally met my associates." He waved the two men forward, who came and stood next to him at the water's edge. The bearded men nodded to the group; one was a bit taller than the other and had wavy black hair that touched his shoulders.

"I am Uriel." He touched his companion's arm. "This is Haniel."

Haniel, who was lighter-skinned with straight brown hair, bowed. "It is an honor to assist you mighty ones with your calling.

"Thank you, my friends," Jesus said to the angels. He continued to brief the team. "We are inside Mount Joy, and this," He gestured to the whole area, "is a world between worlds. Each doorway or portal can bring you to an infinite number of places, times, regions, realms, or spheres. I know you have questions, and I cannot promise you will get all of them answered...at least not today, but you will get some answers. Now, I have a few critical things to show you before you finish what you came to do."

Jesus turned to the edge of the pool and beckoned everyone to join him. As each of them took a place around the pool, it began to glow, changing the light patterns on the cave walls.

"Uriel, Haniel, lead us, please."

The men nodded and dove into the water, disappearing from view. The water was perfectly clear, and the men should have been visible under it if they were still there. Yet, the pool was empty of anything but liquid light.

"Woah!" Lincoln said, "Where'd they go?"

Gianna shook her head, smiling, "Curiouser and curiouser.."

Jesus looked at their stunned faces. "Well, what are you waiting for? Jump in."

Lucy giggled with excitement and jumped in first, promptly disappearing. Gianna looked at Lincoln, shrugged, and dove in. Lincoln followed, with Diego just behind. Billie Jean hesitated, looking a bit nervous. Darrel grabbed her hand in support. "Come on, it's okay."

She nodded weakly, and they jumped in together.

They appeared within seconds of each other in a rolling grassy field with a sparkling stream running through it. The shining sun lightly warmed their skin, and a beautiful breeze with the scent of wildflowers moved through the area. In front of them was a long table, ornately decorated and covered with every delicacy one could imagine. They were shocked to find their armor gone, and they were instead dressed in their "normal" clothing. In particular, Billie Jean was horrified that she was back to being overweight, and she quickly let go of Darrel's hand and turned away in embarrassment. She tried to transform into a lion, but sadly found she could not.

Darrel, aware of her discomfort, took her hand again, "Hey, Billie Jean, I don't care about that. Please don't think I, or any of us, see you any differently."

Gianna nodded and put her hand on Billie Jean's back. "Billie Jean, you are so beautiful! Whoever has put in your head that you aren't beautiful, because of your body shape, is a worthless human being."

Billie Jean shook her head. "Stop, please, both of you. I'm okay. I'm just in shock. I didn't expect to be back in my old body all of a sudden."

The others had already begun to approach the large table, but the angels, Uriel and Haniel, were nowhere in sight, and neither was Yeshua. They approached the overladen table, and each of them spied specific foods that were their favorites. Diego stood in front of a still-steaming plate of steak and potatoes, with a golden goblet of wine in front. Gianna found a plate of spongy yeast rolls with what looked like honey butter and a huge bowl of Italian Wedding soup. Meanwhile, Darrel spotted a giant turkey leg, cornbread stuffing, and spicy sausage and greens. His stomach responded with rumbles of anticipation. Lucy angled for a large bowl of ice cream covered in caramel, nuts, and cherries, while also eyeing a nearby pink cake. And Billie Jean, who stood in front of a plate of chicken fried steak and mashed potatoes covered in gravy, closed her eyes and inhaled the scent in eager expectation. They looked to Diego with a bit of uncertainty.

Lincoln, who had found a plate of chicken parmesan, spoke first. "What do you make of this, Professor? Are we okay to partake of this feast?" he asked with a smile and wink.

"Let us sit and eat, young ones, as we thankfully enjoy what He has prepared for us," Diego answered.

As they pulled out their chairs, suddenly, their eyes were opened. They saw they were surrounded by hundreds of vile creatures, including those who'd previously been defeated: Jezebel and Despair, as well as The Witch King, the harpies, and many other nightmarish beasts.

Panic overcame them. Without their powers and armor, they were defenseless.

Gianna's heart pumped wildly as dark images slammed into her head. She saw the others have similar reactions. She looked over at Diego. His eyes were closed, and he seemed to be controlling his breathing. She focused on Diego and began breathing slowly in through her nose and out of her mouth. Lucy grabbed Gianna's arm and clamped her eyes shut with a squeal of fear. Gianna held her hand. "Lucy, I'm right here. Breathe."

Gianna prayed. *Jesus, help us! Where are you?*

Daughter, I never left you.

Then, why are they here?

Remember what is true. Psalm 23.

Psalm 23. I know this one. I know it.

Her mind was being continuously bombarded with hellacious pictures of gore and death.

Stop!!! She shouted in her head.

She couldn't think. A phrase came through suddenly.

The shadow of death. That was it! Yea, though I walk through the shadow of death! Okay. Yea, though I walk through the valley of death, I will fear no evil; for Thou art with me; thy rod and staff; they comfort me.

Out loud, she spoke, "Thou preparest a table before me in the presence of mine enemies: Thou hast anointed my head with oil, my cup runneth over…!"

Immediately, the dark creatures around her screamed and roared, and the bombardment on their minds faltered, like a record skipping.

Diego heard her and joined in loudly, "Thou preparest a table before me in the presence of mine enemies!" He looked at the team. "Yes! Everyone sit down now and begin to eat!"

They all pulled up their chairs, sat, and began to eat and drink; as they did, the mental onslaught ceased. Their eyes were opened, and around the table were the warrior angels who helped them at the beginning of their journey. They suddenly understood that they were never in danger; they were never alone. Yeshua, Uriel, and Haniel were seated at the front end of the table with them as if they'd been there all along. The Lord and the angels smiled widely, holding up their drink goblets. "My children! Do you see?" He gestured widely with his arms. "I am always with you! Raise your glasses!"

Gianna grabbed her cup in relief and raised it, as did the others.

Jesus looked at each of them tenderly, then prayed, "Father, thank you for setting these apart for Your work. You have kept these truths from the scholars and revealed them to children. Today, you have established them as wise warriors! May Your favor cover them like a shield as you bring Your kingdom into all the earth. L'chaim! To Life!" And as He finished His blessing, He brought the goblet to His lips and drank.

They joyfully raised their glasses, "L'chaim!"

PART 2

CHAPTER 12

Once again, they found themselves in the cave of doorways between worlds. Gianna appreciated feeling her familiar uniform again and gripped her sais with fondness. Jesus addressed the group.

"The enemy is a counterfeit and a chameleon. He cannot create and has no original ideas, but takes from the heavenly kingdom and twists and perverts what We have created. He has many forms, including one that looks exactly like me. Even the Elect will be deceived if they are unprepared and not tuned into the Spirit of Truth. You are about to see much of this first-hand." He looked at Uriel and Haniel and said, "Show them."

The angels transformed before their eyes into stunning creatures whose outer beauty transcended imagination. Each had an opalescent body with muscular flanks that resembled a horse but only in the most base way that a human mind looked for comparison. From the long, muscled back emerged a Roman god-like torso, arms, and head like a man. Gianna's eyes were transfixed.

They're like centaurs.

Finally, out of the horse-like body, unfolded immense multi-colored wings, seemingly made of light. Gianna's chest burst with the glory that radiated from the beings. The depth of understanding of which she began to scratch the surface brought her to her knees, shaking and in tears.

No, nothing like Greek centaurs. Not even close.

"Oh! I get it!" Gianna suddenly said out loud, "The centaurs were a perverted counterfeit of these glorious heavenly beings!"

The Master's voice answered her enthusiastically. "Yes, daughter! You have begun to understand a little. Now, stand up."

Strengthened, she stood, as did the others around her. The sensation of glory slowly waned. Yeshua then transformed into the great Gryphon they had first seen on the mountain. The angelic creatures, Uriel and Haniel, though large in size, were dwarfed by the breathtaking Gryphon.

Gianna's breath caught, as this was the first time she saw the stunning beast up close. He stood before them again, incredible with His enormous multi-colored wings enfolded around His muscular lion body. He crouched low and looked at them with His piercing sapphire eyes.

We can each carry two of you.

The Waking

Gianna didn't wait for anyone and quickly climbed onto the Gryphon's back. Lincoln followed behind her. Darrel and Billie Jean got up on one of the angelic beings with Diego and Lucy on the other. Gianna heard a loud crack, and they all ducked and covered their heads. When nothing fell on them, she looked up. The ceiling of the cave had opened, and grey smoke began pouring out of it.

The Voice penetrated their thoughts clearer than any sound.

The enemy's realm is disorienting. It will take some time to adjust. We will fly around until all of you have adapted, then we will go in for a closer look. You must pay attention to all that you hear and see. You will need to remember as much as possible, because when you come back through to this realm, you may lose some things in the readjustment.

Gianna nodded and noticed Lincoln did the same. She was nervous—it sounded dangerous to go into the enemy's territory. What would happen to them there?

Do not fear, dear one. You will be safe. I Am with you.

She almost slapped herself. Of course! She was with The King of Kings! How could she even fear or doubt?

The Gryphon spread His enormous wings and shot up into the smoky hole. The others followed closely behind.

They flew up for a long time into darkness and foul-smelling smoke. Occasionally, there was a flash of red light that illuminated the long cave, but Gianna couldn't tell where it was coming from. When it happened, she briefly caught a glimpse of the cave walls and the endless tunnel above… or was it below? It felt like they were flying downward even though they had initially gone up through the ceiling of the cave. The feeling of descent was overwhelming.

"Lincoln, are we flying upward or downward?" she asked, after what seemed like hours of traveling.

Lincoln was sitting behind her but hadn't said anything since they'd set out. "Yuh know, I've been wondering that myself. It really does feel like we're going downward. I'm all twisted up in my mind trying to figure it out."

They continued flying into the unending darkness. The discomfort slowly increased as they dealt with the dank-smelling smoke, along with the escalating temperature. Gianna, left to her jittery thoughts, was uncomfortable and nervous. There was no way to tell how long they'd been maddeningly descending upward. Every time the red light flashed, there was hope to see an end to the tunnel, but so far, no end had come to view. She started to become anxious for relief; she wanted out! Out of this infernal, never-ending tunnel with the constant flap of wings, going down into nowhere!

Then thoughts *(were they her own?)* bombarded her head.

Jesus may love you, but it's a strange kind of love that would bring you into such darkness and danger. Is He really going to protect you? He didn't actually tell you beforehand what you would be in for. If you could get more knowledge and understanding for yourself, you wouldn't need Him for protection. You could protect yourself. You deserve better than this.

Gianna's heart suddenly burned with anger. She shook her head. *No, no. That's not true. Oh, God, forgive me. That I would think I could do anything by myself, when I know apart from you, I can do nothing. I love You, and I know You love me. You alone are the victor, and I trust You, my Savior, and My God.*

A warmth suddenly flooded her heart, and the anger left.

Good girl! Yes, that's the way to overcome, daughter!

Just then, they burst through the far mouth of the seemingly endless tunnel and suddenly were flying inside a gigantic cavern, peppered with cave openings all over the walls as far up as they could see. Within the cavern, the atmosphere was grey and dim. There appeared to be no light source except fire pits scattered here and there on the rugged dirt ground. The air was thick and heavy, reeking of sulfur. They struggled, trying not to take too deep of a breath, but they couldn't help wheezing and coughing.

Up ahead, in the middle of the cavern, a great black mountain came into view— the source of the noxious grey smoke. A waterfall of lava sprang from an opening in the middle of the mountain, filling the fiery lake far below, and spewing vast clouds of black and grey. The molten rock surrounding the base flowed like a crimson stream with lava bubbles bursting up here and there in sprays of fiery ooze. As they glided closer, the heat and smell thickened, and sweat dripped off of the travelers. Gianna's eyes grew heavy as she labored to wipe the sweat from them, and each breath seemed a herculean effort. She felt Lincoln fall forward against her back, which startled her out of a hot stupor.

"Lincoln!" she elbowed him.

He moved back, "Oh! Sorry, Gi. . . I am having a heck of a time back here. The heat and smell are just too much."

"I know, I'm struggling too, but the Lord won't let anything happen to us. Hopefully, we'll be landing soon."

They saw three giant, winged creatures flying close to the bottom of the mountain, just above the lava lake. She couldn't quite make out what they were until she saw fire spout from their mouths. The beasts flew slowly, wings flapping noiselessly as they circled the mountain. At that moment, Gianna realized their group must be invisible because they were directly above the dragons, and if they'd been spotted, surely the watch-dogs would have been heading straight for them.

Jutting out from the mountain's peak, a dazzling onyx castle stood like a shiny gem, sporting six tall turrets. The dark beauty of it was simultaneously repelling and alluring.

Gianna presumed this was Lucifer's castle and was unsurprised that the fortress epitomized his arrogance. As they got closer, she saw ornate statues of him in different positions of power carved into the outer walls. One, in particular, made her turn and spit in disgust as it had him standing with his foot on the neck of a mangled figure of Jesus. There were also numerous windows flecked with jewels and gold, particularly thousands of blood-red rubies of every shape and size glinting off every corner, peak, and angle.

Suddenly, there was a familiar hair-raising screech as thousands of black creatures flew out from one of the tallest turrets and began to circle the castle. As they glided closer, Gianna recognized them as the same type of monster that attacked her when she first woke up in the strange world. Lucy called them screechers because of the horrible noise they make. Hearing their clamor a thousand times over was almost unbearable. The avian brood whooshed past them as they got closer, but did not attack. Gianna thought that the creatures might have been sent out because they had been detected, but apparently, that was not the case. In formation, the creatures dove to intercept a large contingent of soldiers of various sizes and shapes approaching the fortress from the ground below.

A massive boom like a thunderclap startled Gianna and Lincoln, causing them to quickly duck and grab tightly to the Gryphon. The black screechers scattered wildly, and all of them quickly rocketed back to the tower from which they came. The dragons had landed in the lava lake and were lounging lazily like swamp alligators, showing no reaction to the boom, and neither did the visitors standing at the lake edge directly in front of the beasts.

The three heavenly beings and the team descended onto a large platform, jutting from the shining palace's side.

The enormous landing area boasted black and gold marble floors, and numerous fiery wall sconces lit up the opulent decor. In the center, providing most of the lighting in the area sat a large hideous sculpture. Carved into the form, at every angle, were human faces in various states of agony, and from the interior of it came multi-colored dark flame.

The travelers dismounted, and Gianna shuddered as she walked past the sculpture. The group followed the Gryphon and angels further into the area until they came within sight of the tallest French doors Gianna had ever seen. They stood against a far wall, where they had a view of the doors and the whole area.

Remember, they cannot see or detect us. Just watch and mark what you observe.

Standing next to the Gryphon and angelic beings gave Gianna and the others some feelings of security in this evil place. She was no longer bothered by the heat and smell, but now felt a dark dread, which made her shiver as if a cold breeze had suddenly hit her bones from the inside. She wished she could be anywhere but here.

Courage, dear heart.

The Gryphon's wing came around her, gently pulled her close, and she instantly felt safe. Lucy quickly scrambled next to her and under His wing as well. Gianna took her hand.

Watch.

There was another deafening thunderclap, shaking the mountain. Then, in a blink, four towering beings stood on the platform just a few feet from Gianna and the others. She swallowed back the bile that rose in her throat at the sight of them.

The French doors swung open, and two immense, black-winged warriors walked out dressed in armor and carrying gleaming spears. They stood, at attention, on either side of the doorway as Lucifer strode in. He was perfectly handsome, eyes completely black and cold, and his beautiful, shining raven hair tied back at the top with the rest falling to his shoulders. He wore a midnight-colored leather uniform, with a golden velvet robe flowing behind him. Strapped to his hip shined a ruby-jeweled sword. Gianna shivered. *Was this really him? The one who had once been the shining angel that covered the very throne of God?* She shook her head, the cold darkness coming from him was almost palpable.

Awaiting him in a semicircle, stood the four armored personages, three brutish and masculine, and the other akin to a female giant with scaly reptilian skin. Satan was taller than the average man, easily close to seven feet, but amazingly, the dark figures on the platform towered over him. They dipped their heads in homage as he entered.

"Baal, what have you to report on our plans?"

The grey-skinned creature who answered had the head and horns of a bull, a thick humanoid body with bulging muscles, and foul coal-black tattoos covering his arms and chest.

"The troops are gathered at the main gate on our side, my Liege, and all our servants have the needed sacrifices in place as well. We await the alignment in fifteen hours to initiate the final phase."

Lucifer cracked a smile. "Excellent. Show me."

A hologram map of the world appeared in the air between them with red dots, highlighting thirteen places on the earth. Gianna saw two in the US, two in Mexico, one in South America, three in Europe, and five in the Middle East, Africa, and Asia. The most prominent dot pulsed brightly in the center of Europe above Italy.

Lucifer examined the map intently. "Your team at Cern..." he arched his eyebrow in Baal's direction, "you're confident they can pull off the final phase?"

"Indisputably."

His thick, sinister voice gave Gianna chills of dread.

"They are prepared to sacrifice their own lives to finish this, if necessary. Of course, my promise that they'll rule with me in the spirit realm for their work assures their full compliance."

He cackled at this, and the others joined in, seemingly enjoying this inside-joke.

"Good! We cannot afford any weak links in this endeavor. We must open every gate, most importantly, the gate at Cern, to release Abaddon and his army and The Pacific Triangle for the release of Leviathan. Without them, we cannot guarantee the annihilation of three-quarters of the human population."

Gianna's mouth dropped open, and she looked at the Gryphon. "Lord, You can't let them get away with this!"

He gently turned her back to the nefarious group. *Hush child, You forget we are here observing everything they're doing. Watch. Listen.*

"My Master, our thirteen teams are ready at the main gate on Mount Woe. They will be released as soon as each portal opens."

Baal touched the map, and the hologram changed to a screen showing a horde, thousands of giants of various sizes and colors. "This is the first team out," he smiled horribly revealing rows of shark-like fangs. "*My* sons! Set to go through gate number one on Peak Kailash in Tibet. And here are the others."

The screen changed as he went through and highlighted one ghastly team after another of various beasts, monsters, and creatures that they planned to release into the physical world to murder, rape, and pillage. Tears poured from Gianna's eyes as she repeated the names when she saw them. In order: Peak Kailash, Tibet; Ziggurat of Ur, Iraq; Mount Hermon, Lebanon/Syria; Nubian Pyramids, Sudan; Stonehenge, Uk; Vatican, Rome; Washington Monument, DC; Pyramid of the Sun, Mexico; Pyramids of Tikal, Guatemala; Machu Picchu, Peru; The Devil's Triangle, Pacific Ocean; Cern, Switzerland. The screen focused on the last team, which consisted of a rather large group of particularly wicked-looking giants, not too unlike the ugly orcs from *The Lord of the Rings* movies, but these looked much bigger and meaner.

"As you ordered, the Cern gate will have a team of Nephil warriors, who will be Abaddon's elite guard when he is released. Of course, The Destroyer has his own army awaiting the opening, but these 100 are particularly deadly and have been bred and trained specifically for his service."

Lucifer stroked his chin as he observed this last group. "Yes! They *are* impressive! I will go myself to meet them. I want to look at these warriors in person, as well as be there to welcome my brother when he comes out. It's been millennia since we've seen one another. I am eager for his arrival."

"Master, Oceanus awaits you as well at the Pacific Gate for Leviathan's release. He fears the Ancient beast will go its own way rather than being steered."

Satan pursed his lips, looking annoyed but thoughtful. "Pitiful, weak fool, he was always inept. Poseidon would have never asked for help! Damn that Michael! He's got much vengeance coming his way for taking down one of my strongest princes! Wait until he sees what will become of his precious Jerusalem!"

He grinned and rubbed his hands together with the thought. Baal cleared his throat. Lucifer arched an eyebrow, annoyed.

"Oceanus, Master?"

"Ah, yes," he frowned. "The fool. He's probably correct that he isn't able to handle his task."

He walked over to the giant with long squid tentacles for hair and beard, and four thick muscled arms that ended in flippered appendages.

"Dagon."

The aquatic giant bowed, "Yes, my king?" His voice had a strange underwater quality to it.

"You, fish god, will go in my stead and assist him. If all goes well, there could be a huge promotion in it for you."

Dagon again bowed his head, "Thank you, My Liege."

Lucifer, hands clasped behind his back, walked over to the female creature. "Inanna, have your scouts seen any sign the Enemy is going to hinder our move?"

Her yellow reptilian eyes focused on Satan, then she bowed slightly before answering. "My Lord, no counter-move has been detected thus far. We have thousands of eyes and ears watching the heavenly hosts and any possible prophetic discerners. The Enemy has, however, been giving his people dreams and they are . . . interceding—"

"I assume you have assignments on these intercessors around the clock. We cannot allow effective prayer to interfere with our plans." He sounded agitated.

"Of course, Master. Our best agents are at work: Lust,

Distraction, Pride, Bitterness, Offense, Chaos...the heavens have been closed like iron doors above the...*prayer warriors.*"

She emphasized those two words with a mocking tone, then cackled, revealing long pointed fangs behind blood-red lips. Inanna was muscular and thick and oozed seduction and cruelty. Her curvy body was accentuated by a shiny, black-armored bodice and short chainmail, leather skirt.

He scowled and stood inches from her, causing her cackling to stop abruptly. "Inanna, this is our chance to get the upper hand on Him. By depleting the human population, except for what we need as food and slaves, and filling the world with our hybrids, we will thwart His plan to save any more of them. We've worked for centuries for everything to align perfectly!"

He grabbed the giant reptilian by her throat and pinned her to the rock as though she weighed nothing. She squirmed but made no move to fight him.

"If I find out that you haven't done every detail that I have commanded, you will suffer...and it will be my pleasure to watch you slowly burn for it."

She gasped but managed to wheeze out, "Yes, Master,

I have planned for every contingency... but you must know it is The Almighty we are dealing with, there is nothing that we can truly hide from Him."

He pulled her back and pummeled her twice against the rock, which broke into several giant pieces. He slammed her onto the ground and yelled, "I don't accept your excuses, goddess of war and sex! I certainly know WHO I AM DEALING WITH! DO YOU PRESUME TO LECTURE ME ABOUT THE ALMIGHTY?" He spit on the ground after saying the name, "Do you forget, *god-dess*, that I AM LUCIFER! THE COVERING CHERUB!!?

He released her, stood up, and smoothed his hair. Then he approached the last one calmly, disregarding his maniacal outburst. Inanna stayed on the ground for a while afterward, groaning quietly to herself.

"Osiris? What have you to report? I'm especially interested in these 'chosen' warriors Yeshua is training."

The giant with green skin and an Egyptian pharaoh's headdress spoke up.

"Master, that was my task." He nodded his head stiffly in homage. "My scouts have reported that they have spent quite some time, of late, inside Mount Joy." His voice was so gruff and low that, when he spoke, Gianna felt the sound rumble through her like a stereo base.

"Go on."

"They most definitely are in the company of The Word, and also Uriel and Haniel. They were seen entering the cave of worlds, but...uh..."

"BUT, UH? COME ON! OUT WITH IT!"

The green-skinned god hesitated. "Our scouts were prevented from following further because the heavenly host were guarding the entrance."

Lucifer said nothing, but his face was a volcano before eruption. He practically whispered, "I must be dealing with imbeciles." He then exploded. "ARE WE NEWBORNS OR ARE WE GODS!?!" he thundered.

Osiris' elaborately painted facial features remained stony and emotionless amid the outburst.

Lucifer pointed up into Osiris' statuesque face, "When, pray tell, were you going to offer this information, so I could get my stealth forces to work?"

"I assumed you would want to hear this information directly from me, Master." Osiris rumbled deeply.

The interplay between the two intrigued Gianna, though she was a bit panicked that they were discussing her team. Her inquisitiveness took over, and she was wondering what kind of power play was occurring between the dark prince and one of his top generals here.

Satan turned his back to the giant Pharaoh, his brow knit in a deep scowl. As he momentarily stepped away from the generals, he closed his eyes and cracked his neck as if trying to relax and think. All of a sudden, he opened his eyes—which had transformed into yellow reptilian orbs—and his mouth suddenly became a razor filled maw, his neck extending out serpent-like, and his voice morphing into something from a dark pit. He looked back at Osiris, "Even Death will be thrown into the lake of fire on Judgement Day, god of death!"

The Dark Lord then called to his guard, "GET MY STEALTH TEAM!"

Gianna and the others who had screamed or covered their ears when Satan changed, were quickly swept up onto their hosts, and before they knew it, they were flying out of the fortress and back up the dark tunnel. The further they flew away from the dark kingdom, the more the fear and panic left their hearts and minds.

CHAPTER 13

Back at the pool's edge in the cave of worlds, the team sat in stunned silence. Many of them gazed listlessly at the waves of color dancing on the walls. The Griffon and the angelic beings stood amongst the warriors and slowly flapped their wings—reminiscent of the angel warriors who had helped the team early on in their journey. Inhaling the light and fragrant breeze, each of them began to feel the bleakness slowly lift from them like a mist clearing when the sun bursts through the clouds.

"The atmosphere from the enemy's realm tends to linger. You will soon feel yourselves again, my children," Yeshua said as he and the angels changed back into human form.

Finally, Diego, still looking a bit troubled, stood and approached his Master. "Lord, You alone know the hearts of men, and You alone can test them. Please grant us the grace for the task before us, as I admit this seems too great for our feeble bodies of flesh." He sounded so childlike and forlorn that Gianna felt her eyes well up.

The Lord gently placed his hands upon Diego's shoulders, "My son, this is exactly why you will succeed. You understand that you can do nothing of yourselves." He smiled tenderly, "Your request is granted."

He turned back to the others. Although he had taken the form of a humble traveler again, his sea-colored eyes captivated any who engaged Him. "Come, warriors." He began walking out of the cave and gestured for them to follow. "I'm so excited for you to see what we have in store for you."

Jesus led them back to the clearing at the top of Mount Joy. "It is my pleasure to inform you that now that you have been hardened by experience, We have enhanced your abilities."

There was an excited murmur amongst them. Gianna was already so impressed with her skill set; she couldn't imagine needing or wanting anything more.

Jesus stepped first over to the Seer, placing his hand on him. "Diego, your staff has been enhanced and is now capable of multiple functions, which you will discover as you use it." Diego looked curiously at his staff and walked off smiling, intending to experiment with it right away.

Jesus then looked at Gianna, "Daughter, you now have

two offensive weapons: short swords sheathed at your back along with the skill for use."

He grinned at Lucy, who looked down and giggled. "Darrel and Lucy," He placed a hand on both of them, "you both now have the gift of flight." Darrel looked like a kid getting exactly what he wanted for Christmas. "Yes! Let's go!" Darrel yelled as he pumped his fist in the air.

Next, Jesus rested his hand on Lincoln. "Lincoln, you can harden your body when fighting, and no bullet or blade can penetrate it." The warrior bowed his head. "Thank you, Lord."

Lastly, He walked over to Billie Jean and gave her arm a gentle squeeze. "And dear daughter, you can now transform into a gryphon for battle. Your roar can shake mountains and resonates at a frequency that many dark enemies cannot endure."

His joy was tangible as He bestowed the new gifts. Straightaway, they began to test their new enhancements.

Darrel's whole body became a flame, and he shot up into the air like a rocket. Lucy cautiously floated three feet off the ground and simply moved forward slowly. Diego's staff was imbued with power, similar to Moses' staff, but more battle-ready; so far, he discovered it could light up in dark places, transform into a snake or rope, and when tapped to the ground, cause a short distance earthquake.

Gianna pulled the beautiful swords from sheathes at her back. The slightly curved silver blades had ornate gold designs on them, and like her sais, they felt made for her with perfect weight and balance. She tried them out with a few slashes and flips and was very pleased with the outcome. Her sais were more defensive weapons, and these swords were definitely for offensive fighting. Lincoln stood in front of her. "Try to cut me."

She smirked playfully and attacked him with spin kicks and multiple slashes, which he blocked easily with his hardened arms resulting in a sound like blades hitting metal. "Impressive!" She remarked.

Billie Jean transformed into a stunning white gryphon, a bit smaller than Jesus' Gryphon. She had powerful, large talons, a golden beak and eyes, muscular lion's body, and an incredible wingspan. The Lord changed into His Gryphon and let out a ground-shaking screech. Billie Jean responded with a powerful call of her own, and they took off in flight. The group watched, transfixed, as the two marvelous creatures interacted in a flying dance of spins, flips, and dives.

Soon, they returned and simultaneously transformed

upon landing. Jesus and Billie Jean walked back toward the others arm in arm. He smiled at her, "You were wonderful!"

The group gathered around them, clapping and whooping their amazement.

"I have another surprise for you all!" Jesus said to them, grinning with excitement. Immediately, a young man appeared at the Lord's side. He was thick, muscular, and ruggedly handsome, with curly reddish-brown hair and a short beard. Jesus bear-hugged him, and they both laughed joyfully.

"This is King David, the Giant Slayer! He is here to train and lead you to the victorious destruction of the enemy's plan!"

Diego, like a starry-eyed schoolboy, approached him. "King David! You're my hero! Your courage! Your faith! Your heart for God! Even while we've been here fighting through our trials, your Psalms have been anchors for us in overcoming and withstanding the enemy!"

David embraced him like an old friend. "Diego, I'm humbled and thrilled at your words, and to be asked to help you all with this endeavor!" He addressed the group. "You were born for such a time as this! Heaven is watching you all at the edge of their seats!"

Gianna tried to wrap her mind around Heaven watching them and that this crazy adventure was part of their destiny. The fate of the world seemed to be hanging in the balance. What if they failed? Would she let the Lord and the whole world down?

She must have shown the doubt on her face because David remarked, "Don't be troubled, warriors. Take it from someone who's had his epic failures displayed in Scripture for thousands of years." He put his hand on his chest. "Your heavenly Father knows what you will and won't do, good and bad, and still puts you to the assigned task." He looked directly at Gianna. "Is there someone better qualified? Possibly." He stared at Lincoln, "Is the Maker of the Universe worried about you flubbing up His plan? Doubtful." He placed his hand gently on Lucy's, and she shyly looked down. "His will for each of you is to become what He designed you to be...ultimately, as much like Our Master as possible."

The team felt a bit less anxious as David encouraged them. He smiled at them, his brown eyes dancing with joy. "Hey, guess what? No matter what happens today, Lucifer will still end up in the Lake of Fire. So, nothing he does will stop that. Today, we're just going to make all of those hundreds of years of plans get so wasted that he won't be able to turn that frown upside down for a loooong time. It will be EPIC!" He fist-bumped Jesus at that, and they both laughed.

The team also started laughing at the display.

"I love giving that guy a bad day!" Jesus snickered.

"How about a bad century?!" Lincoln added.

"Yeah, let's destroy that loser!" Shouted Lucy.

They all began to join in on the exciting banter.

Finally, David interjected, "Okay, Okay. Let's calm down now and focus." David gestured for them to come closer. "Pay close attention, because even though you all are enhanced, you can still get hurt and die. Your survival is imperative for future plans. I'm going to instruct you on the strengths and weaknesses of your opponents. Specifically, how to kill a giant...or, in your case, *many* giants."

CHAPTER 14

"So, what you're sayin' is, I can burn one of those nasty things to a crisp, and it won't die?"

"Darrel, I am glad you asked that." David hammered his fist into his hand and looked at each of them. "I must emphasize emphatically, that NOTHING will kill a ne-phil except cutting its head off or stabbing it completely through the heart. Whenever possible, do both." David had just begun instructing them about giants, and the team had many questions. "These creatures are worse than your fictional vampires. They are big, strong, smelly, and smart! They are half-god! Also, they each have special abilities; some can even immobilize you with their thoughts."

Lincoln, eyes wide, asked, "King David, how are just the six of us going to stand a chance against the thousands of giants and other monsters if what you're saying is true?"

"Please, little brother, just call me David." David waved his hand calmly. "Look, all of you, let us backtrack. If we can help it, you will not be going toe-to-toe against this whole dark army. You are merely 'throwing a wrench in the machine,' so to speak. Will you be fighting some bad guys? Yes, very likely. Some really wretched giants and ugly beasts? Most definitely. But no need to fear, when heaven is on your side!"

"Okay...Okay...so can we get down to the nitty-gritty on this, *friend?* How are we . . ." Darrel began to count the team, "Nine! ... going to stop 13 gates of hell from opening up?!"

"Yes, please tell me, we just have to flip a switch or steal a key or something?" quipped Lucy.

Gianna laughed nervously. "I'm sure it's something like that, right? Then the whole angel army will come in and destroy Satan's armies?"

David put his hands up. "Listen, I know this is a lot to take in, but I'm not going to sugarcoat any of it for you. It's an incredibly daunting task. Firstly, no, there is no ring or key or switch that will just shut the gates. We have specific assignments that will be difficult and horrifying. But our tasks are ALL that we focus on. We will have *some* help from the heavenly host, but there will be no angel army coming to save the day in this scenario."

"WHAT?!" They all shouted in unison.

"Where is Jesus? Can we ask Him about all this?" Darrel demanded, "I'm pretty sure this hasn't been thoroughly thought out."

"Our *Lord*," David emphasized, " has other matters to attend to and, I can assure you, Darrel, He has most definitely thought this out." He chuckled as he ran his hand through his auburn curls. "Friends, please give me a chance to explain, and you will understand . . . at least the first part."

Gianna sighed in frustration but kept quiet so David could finish.

"The first part is vital. You will see many horrible, ugly things happening to people that you will not be able to do anything about. You must focus only on your assigned task. These certain things must be accomplished, so do not get distracted." He paused and looked at each of them. "Listen carefully and understand, there is power in human blood, and specific blood rituals will be done to open these gates. That being said, these are our main objectives: Objective #1..."

He held up one finger. "There is a young girl at the 13th gate at Cern who must be saved before she is sacrificed. She is 11-years-old, and her name is Amora. Without her, Abaddon the Destroyer cannot be freed, and he is a main concern at this point. He must not be released before the appointed time."

He held up two fingers. "Objective #2... at the 12th gate, turn Leviathan against the enemy. Leviathan is a horrific, dangerous entity, but has never obeyed a master, and can cause devastating chaos. It has been restrained by The Most High for thousands of years, but the enemy seeks to release it and use it to lay waste to many seafaring islands and countries. So, the enemy's plan to free it can definitely work in our favor."

He held up three fingers. "Objective #3... keep as many nefarious entities on this side of the portals as possible. The easiest way, since we can't be in 13 places at once, is to do it from this side. Once they get through, it will be virtually impossible to bring them back in."

Gianna and Lincoln looked at David blankly. Darrel, hands on hips, stared at the ground, shaking his head and muttered, "...crazy..."

And Lucy shrugged, "I don't get it."

"Young ones," Diego addressed the group, "let David finish explaining. I'm sure we will grasp the fullness of the plan better once he does."

David continued as if they were all on board and sharply focused. "I'm splitting us up into three teams and assigning each team an objective. Team number one: Uriel,

Gianna, and Lucy. Team number two: Haniel, Lincoln, and Diego. Team number three: Darrel, Billie Jean, and myself."

"So, I assume my team will take Objective one to save the girl?" asked Gianna.

He pointed at Gianna and grinned, "Correct! Your team saves Amora, Diego's team turns Leviathan against the enemy, and my team keeps the enemy on the dirty side of the portal and destroys as many as possible!"

Darrel very calmly walked over to David with his hands on his hips, "You, me, and Billie Jean are going to hold back thousands of monsters and giants for however long," he shrugged and pointed to David. "You ain't gonna' die because you're already dead. She and I gotta' manage to not get dead somehow." He shrugged sarcastically again. "Oh yeah. I'm sure this is doable."

David's eyes sparkled, and he winked at Darrel. "Trust me, little brother, this is not my first rodeo. I have got us covered." He looked behind them as three figures approached the group. "I did manage to secure some extra muscle for our team."

The first was a muscled, jolly man with bright blue eyes who reminded Gianna of Santa Clause if he was a weight-lifter instead of having a cookie addiction. He was about six-foot-tall with a white beard, but youthful features, sporting light armor and a short thick sword. The other two made him look small. They were at least 8 or 9 feet tall, fully-armed angelic warriors with spears and swords. They were majestic, with perfect features, and beautiful, muscled bodies. The first was ebony-skinned with striking silver eyes, sporting long braids with colors woven in; the other had long, red hair and a full, thick beard, with green eyes.

David and the white-bearded man clasped forearms and greeted each other warmly. The angel warriors nodded stoically with slight grins. Uriel and Haniel, who'd been mostly quiet until the visitors arrived, also embraced 'super Santa' warmly—whose eyes brightened in return.

"Uriel, my old friend!" the man said. "It's been ages! Always on the most exciting assignments, I see?"

"Ah, Noah! Can anything be as exciting as battling first-generation nephil beside such a warrior as yourself?"

"I'm eager to be back in the game after all this time!" Noah whooped heartily.

David steered his attention over to the team. "Noah, please meet our young warriors!"

"Yes, introduce me, brother!" He gestured to the team,

his muscular arms bulging. "What an incredible, ferocious group you all are!"

Lucy giggled, and he winked and smiled warmly at her. Gianna thought of Santa again and laughed.

"Team, this is the legendary Noah ben Lamech, the very man who built the ark before the Great Deluge. What you may not know is what a ruthless and formidable giant slayer he was in his day!"

"Ha! Really in *all* days! Those puny things you fought weren't even a true challenge, David. Right, Uriel?" Noah elbowed the angel.

Uriel and Haniel both laughed. Gianna delighted in seeing real personality come from the angels for the first time since they'd joined the group. She also really enjoyed the mood that Noah evoked.

David put his hands on his hips and shook his head. "He's always giving me a hard time because the Giants were so much bigger before the flood."

Noah put his hand on Uriel's back. "Uriel, remember that 40-footer we brought down in the Kidron Valley?"

"I believe it was 36 feet . . ." corrected Uriel.

Noah winked and shrugged. "36 . . .40, what's the

difference when it gets that tall, right?" He looked at the group. "The monster was coming down from the mountains and devouring whole towns of people, just slaughtering them. It was horrible. Uriel and I --"

"Brother," David interrupted, "I am sure they would love to hear your adventures, but we have much to discuss with the current tasks."

Noah humphed playfully. "He just doesn't like to hear about fighting *real* giants; those 10 footers he and his men brought down were just another day at the office for us."

The team enjoyed Noah's jovial character and was very impressed with meeting such a legendary figure. Diego expressed his disappointment at not being able to hear more of Noah's stories. David again emphasized their need to move forward but promised a time of hearing the "old man's tall tales" after they accomplished their goals.

He then gestured to the other two angels. "Adonai has also sent us these two mighty warriors second only to Michael himself, Raphael and Raguel. Both have taken down thousands of monsters and giants, but they also were with Uriel and Michael when they bound and imprisoned the worst of the fallen rebel Watchers, Azazel and Samyaza."

The ebony one stepped forward and bowed, "I am

Raphael. We are very pleased to assist you, mighty warriors, with the daunting task ahead. I understand that we are assigned to David's team to hold back the hordes from breaching the gates into the physical earth realm."

"Ay, we're eager for the brawl. It's been too long since our spears have tasted nephil blood!" Raguel expressed with an amusing Scottish lilt. He then stepped forward with a bow, "Raguel, at yer service!"

Hovering a few feet above Raphael, Darrel launched multiple fireballs at the angel. At high speed and with little effort, Raphael deflected the fireballs, jumped, grabbed Darrel by the ankle, and slammed him into the ground like a football after a touchdown.

Darrel moaned in agony. "What'd you do that for, man?!"

Raphael looked down at him shaking his head. "You will die fighting giants in this manner."

"Not if you kill me first!" Darrel shouted back as he slapped Raphael's hand away when offered to help him up.

David offered his hand, which Darrel took after laying there a bit longer—more from anger than pain. "Brother,

Raphael took it easy on you compared to what those monsters can do. It will take a lot more than throwing fire at them." David tapped the side of his own head. "We must fight smarter, rather than harder."

Darrel shook his head and growled. "I just got this power a couple days ago, man, I'm not a trained giant killer! This is just ridiculous to even expect us to know what we're doin' here!"

"I understand your concerns, little brother."

Noah, who had been watching nearby, chimed in. "We really don't want you to try to go head to head against a nephil. You probably would die if you did, actually. But what we want you to grasp is how they move, how fast they are, and, really, how to survive."

"What, exactly, will Billie Jean and I be doing in this plan if we're not directly fighting?"

"Look, you may need to fight if it gets down to that," explained David, "but you and Billie Jean will mostly be running interference while the rest of us kill and keep as many away from the gate openings as possible until the gates close."

"How long will the gates be opened?"

Noah and David looked at each other with raised brows. Noah thought hard for a bit before he answered. "To tell you the truth, we don't really know. . . all dimensional portals are different. They've been preparing most of these gate areas for centuries, and because they're being opened at this time of year, when the veil is thinner, and using blood rituals, they may be opened for longer than average."

Darrel rubbed his bald head. "Okay, then please explain the average."

David answered, "Averages are usually a couple of hours, but the people involved in these gate jobs are the highest-ranking Satanic priests and priestesses on the earth. They do not make mistakes, and they are overachievers—if you know what I mean. They overdo everything, so if the ritual calls for one sacrifice, they will do three. Does that make sense?"

"So, what you're saying is, these portals could stay open for eight or ten hours?"

"Well... actually, what I am saying is it could be days rather than hours."

"WHAT?!" Darrel exploded. "Are you serious, man!?"

Darrel's rant was interrupted as he caught sight of Billie Jean's gryphon flying towards them with Raguel. She landed, transformed, and skipped over to them in apparent excitement. "Hey!" She grabbed Darrel's arm, and he suddenly forgot why he was angry. "I just learned so much about how a gryphon fights and flies at the same time! It was amazing!"

"Ya! She's quite brilliant with 'er wings and claws, that one! I think she'll do just fine weavin' and dodgin' in a dog fight!" quipped Raguel, who was smiling like a proud coach with a star player.

Meanwhile, across the way, Haniel, Diego, and Lincoln gathered for their training. Haniel's silvery-white hair and eight-foot muscular frame astounded Diego and Lincoln when he first walked up. Once Raphael and Raguel joined the group, Uriel and Haniel had transformed from the average bearded travelers, whom the group had come to know, to another of their apparent heavenly forms. Diego made meticulous mental notes of all he'd observed thus far of the angelic beings they had encountered. He longed to sit one of them down and pepper them with dozens of questions.

Haniel smiled kindly down at Diego as if he knew his

thoughts. "I promise when this is all over, we will talk, my friend."

Lincoln raised his eyebrows. "Did I miss something?"

Diego smiled and shook his head, "Oh, Haniel is reading my mind."

"Gotcha."

Haniel held one long red-tipped, gold-shafted spear in each hand. He handed one to each of them. Diego was surprised at the lightness of it; a toddler could wield it with ease.

"These were crafted in heaven, made with exquisite precision, and imbued with glory from the throne of the Almighty. Nothing in the universe can bend or break them. You will also notice that these spears are tipped with red sapphire."

Lincoln whistled, "Wo! Can I keep it when we're done?"

Haniel smiled and winked. "I'm sorry, no, hopefully, the business end of it will be planted deep in the chest of a fallen watcher by the time *you're* done."

Lincoln's eyes were saucers.

"As I was saying, the red sapphire tips illuminate on command, which is essential to our plan of wrangling the sea monster Leviathan. Go ahead and speak to the spears."

"What do we say? Hey, spear, light up?" asked Lincoln.

And to his surprise, the bejeweled tip lit up hugely, casting red light on the whole mountain top. The other groups, who had been busily training yards away, all stopped and looked at the spear in amazement.

"Now tell it to turn off."

"Spear, turn off." The light immediately went out.

Diego also practiced turning his spear on and off. Then, Haniel had them practice throwing them as well, which both men thought was much easier than it should have been.

"Amazing! It's as if the spears hit the targets no matter how they are thrown," remarked Diego.

Haniel nodded. "Actually, they are controlled by sight and thought. As long as the wielder can see the target, he will hit it 100% of the time."

"Man, you have got to let me keep this, Haniel!" Lincoln yelled, his excitement causing the other groups to pause and turn their way again.

Haniel ignored him. "Okay, both of you gather here; let's discuss the details of the plan."

"Please explain what exactly the enemy plans to do with Leviathan, and how only the three of us are to stop this great beast—as well as the gods who want to unleash it on our world," inquired Diego.

As the sunlight reflected briefly off of Haniel's silver eyes, they seemed to flash. Diego also noticed the angel's voice had a musical timbre that made it delightful to listen to. "Leviathan, the great sea dragon, has no master and cannot be tamed. But that sly serpent, Lucifer, seeks to release the beast from its chains in the deep so that it will destroy and cause much chaos to the world of men. Just before The Deluge, the Almighty caged Leviathan in an ether realm between worlds to keep it from attacking Noah's ark, and also to protect his future descendants from its tumultuous wrath. Satan has commissioned Oceanus and Dagon to open the portal at the Devil's Triangle and turn the beast, first, towards the Far East and then on to annihilate the South Pacific Islands."

"How are they able to control where the monster goes?" asked Lincoln.

"Similarly to how we plan to redirect it. Have you ever seen a bullfight?"

"I'm familiar, yes," answered Diego. Lincoln nodded

in agreement.

Haniel took up one of the spears. "The sea dragon will follow red light. It's a fail-safe built into it by Creator. Even though there was never a mate created for Leviathan, it always seeks one. The red flame drives it forward and, thinking it has found a mate, it will give chase. "

"Brilliant," said Diego, nodding his head.

"The enemy is planning to allow it to chase them to the places they want it to destroy, because the longer it chases, the angrier it becomes, and, therefore, the more destruction occurs." Haniel handed the spear to Diego. "Here's our simple plan: after they free Leviathan, I will distract them, and you will pin them to the ocean floor with your spears, allowing the monster to catch them. After it devours the enemy, I will lead it down into the deep with my spear, to a cavern prepared by The Almighty. It will rest there until He releases it again."

Gianna, Lucy, and Uriel stood at the pool in the cave of worlds.

"We must stay focused. You may see dark practices in which you will want to intervene, but our only task is to get the girl out and get her to the prepared safe house. Now, I am about to teach you a new skill, which will be imperative to accomplishing our goal. This is a skill that many believers of the past possessed but has been mostly lost over time. In the near future, many will come to acquire it again. You two will help some of them do that. This skill is called spirit travel; another word for it is 'translation'."

"Is that like astral projection? I tried that once, and it was creepy, and I never tried again," said Lucy.

"No." Uriel shook his head. "Not at all like astral projection, which is of the enemy and is forbidden."

Lucy blew her cheeks out, shrugged, and looked embarrassed.

He gave her a reassuring side hug and continued, "Translation is traveling in the spirit realm from one location to another: body, soul, and spirit. Nothing is left behind. . . and this is accomplished by Ruach, the Holy Spirit himself. Have you read the story of Philip and the Ethiopian Eunuch in the book of Acts, Chapter 8?"

"Oh, I know that one," Gianna nodded, "Philip was a follower of Yeshua, and he overheard a man in a chariot reading from the book of Isaiah. So, Philip asked the man if he understood what he was reading. The man said 'no' and invited Philip into the chariot to explain it to him." Gianna began to gesture with her hands as she got more enthusiastic about the story. "Philip used the Scripture the man was reading to tell him about Messiah. The man believed and asked Philip to baptize him in the river they were traveling near. Philip baptized him, and as soon as it happened, Philip disappeared and reappeared somewhere else to preach the gospel! I was always fascinated by that story."

Uriel smiled. "Yes! That's it. Philip was translated to a city miles away, instantly, by the Holy Spirit." He snapped his fingers. "This is actually a skill that can be developed by believers to accomplish The Most High's will in the earth. It has been used by many believers in the past to minister the gospel and, in some situations, escape persecution and capture. There are actually still some current believers who know it and use it, but the Almighty is releasing it once again to His Elect in these last days."

"Wow, really?" Lucy's eyes were huge with surprise.

"So, that's not something cool that only people in the Bible got to do?" Gianna asked, already excited and beginning to think of scenarios of where she would translate.

Uriel chuckled. "Now, this is not a means of sightseeing and world travel. Ruach will only take you to where you will accomplish His will."

"Aw, man! Can't we help people in Orlando, Florida? And. . . just pass by Disney before we zap out?" Lucy giggled.

He smiled at her and continued, "While we are in Switzerland, we will be dealing with advanced security systems and personnel. In order to evade these obstacles, translation is a must. It is not difficult to do, but it is hard to learn for many humans because you must bypass your logic and reason. This is completely a spirit task; therefore, you must tap into your connection to Ruach through your own spirit."

"Isn't that what we do when we pray?" Asked Gianna.

"Yes, but more so, because you...and many believers... are easily distracted and break connection to Spirit frequently in prayer. You cannot allow a breaking through distraction. Let's begin by practicing your ability to focus."

"Focus. Got it."

"Okay, now each individual focuses differently. Some need to close their eyes, some to sit, some to kneel. Get into your personal position where you are most focused."

Lucy sat, crossed her legs, and closed her eyes. Gianna stood where she was. Uriel looked at her and arched his eyebrow.

"I actually concentrate better standing and with my eyes open. I do my best praying when I walk, actually."

"That's fine. I just wanted to be sure you understood the instructions."

"Perfectly," she nodded.

"Okay then. Bring to your mind a picture of a donut with pink icing and sprinkles. Do you see it?"

"Yup!"

"Yes."

"Wonderful! Now picture an elephant with a tiny blue hat on."

Lucy giggled.

"I'm guessing you see that too? Did either of you have difficulty with those pictures?"

They both answered no.

"Okay. Now think of our Master, Yeshua. Once you have a picture of Him in your minds, put yourself in the scene, and imagine a place that you would like to meet with

Him. Like in a garden or walking by a lake. Your task is to stay in this scene as long as possible without giving in to any distractions here. Stay connected."

Gianna took a deep breath in and out and relaxed. She started by concentrating on the lights from the colored waters dancing on the cave walls. Then, in her mind's eye, began to see her Beloved Master walking towards her. She was standing on a white-sanded beach with her feet at the point where the waves came in, touching her toes, then quickly moving back out. She was wearing a simple blue beach dress with white designs streaking through it and bare feet. The smell of the salty air came in from a soft ocean breeze. She gazed down the shore, and Yeshua was walking toward her, grinning hugely, eyes sparkling with life, his raven curls blown back by the wind. He was wearing loose white cotton pants rolled up to the knees, and a white cotton shirt with sleeves rolled up to the elbows, His bare feet walking through the shallow water. When He was almost to her, she was startled by the obviously visible hole at the top of each foot. Suddenly, the vision from her confrontation with Jezebel came flooding back.

"Gianna, look at Me," He said as He gently took her hand.

She looked into his eyes, the waves moving over their feet, and He melted Her with love; the memory dissipated. He embraced her, and she held on for dear life.

"Don't make me go back. Please, I just want to stay here with You." She whispered into his shoulder.

"This is not withheld from you, child. You can be with Me any time. Your imagination is the key to this dimension."

She looked thoughtful, "Is this going to help me, um, spirit travel?"

"Yes, right now you are learning Focus, and--"

A wave of cold water splashed over Gianna. She yelped and was instantly back in the cave, dripping with water. Uriel was swimming around in the pool, apparently after jumping in and splashing both herself and Lucy. They both looked at the angel in exasperation.

"Uriel?!" Gianna yelled, "How am I supposed to focus with all of this?"

He laughed and swam towards her, "Gianna, that's the point! Focus! Don't disconnect no matter what's going on in the physical realm."

"Oh, that makes sense! So, if someone is about to stab

me, I'm not supposed to disconnect," she stated sarcastically.

He smiled and paddled back towards them. "Again!" he instructed as he stepped out. "Breathe and focus."

CHAPTER 15

Amora sat up on the thin cot, straining to hear the muffled voices in heated converse outside her tiny room. It had been days since she had slept more than an hour or two put together. Nervous that the end of her life was fast approaching, as each day and hour passed, Amora could only overthink, hope, and pray. Two days ago, she had been taken from the large, cold cell that held more than twenty other children of various ages, children she had grown attached to and desired to protect. But how would she, almost dead, save them? The feeling that she had to find a way to escape, and get them out too, overwhelmed her thoughts.

Weeks earlier, Amora was never allowed direct contact with the other children, the ones they kept alive for a time, and then slated for sacrifice. She saw them being led into the rituals, shaking, some screaming in fear, and naked. She'd learned to disconnect a long time ago, to mentally go somewhere else while her body was forced to participate in wicked, dark ceremonies. Amora was the eldest daughter of the high priest and had been groomed from birth to move up in leadership and eventually become the coven's high-priestess.

When she turned eleven, they had amped up the amount and frequency of the mental and sexual abuse to the point that she always thought the next ritual or event would be her last. Each time, she thought maybe she would be allowed to die and be released from the hell on earth that was her life. At times, she could escape into her mind, and something else took over her body. She would wake up in her bed the next day with no memory of the previous night's events. Yet, there was no escaping the misery. Sometimes, even many days later, it was still painful to use the bathroom. The last time though, she remembered every detail. That was the night her death sentence was pronounced.

It had been only two nights after a particularly horrific and painful experience, and Amora was frustrated and angry that she was, yet again, being dressed in black robes. She made the mistake of asking, "Why, again, so soon?" Her answer was a hard slap to the face from her father that knocked her to the ground, briefly blackening her vision. She held her face and looked up, feeling rage welling deep within her belly.

He pointed down at her and yelled, "Shut your mouth,

whore! Another word, and we'll bring you to the meeting on a stretcher!" Her two younger sisters were visibly shaking but uttered nothing. She quickly got up, and they all followed her father out.

She hated him more than anyone, even the awful men and women who seemed to delight in abusing her more than any other child. She hated him deeply and utterly because he offered up her and her sisters so freely. Her sisters, ages nine and seven, also got the worst of it, with lines of horrid men waiting their turn with each of them. Amora began to break protocol and started to resist when her sisters became increasingly forced to participate. It was easier for her to mentally check out when the girls weren't there, but their screams constantly brought her back. Having to watch their suffering, ignited a rebellious fire in Amora that grew with each dark event.

They were brought to a new location that night. A fairly new church in town that was gaining many new Christian converts. Her father had quickly gotten a member of the coven into the congregation, who, soon after, became a volunteer child care worker, and then eventually a paid staff member. It wasn't long before this individual had a key to the facility. They planned to completely desecrate and curse the entire place with blood and sex rituals, which would bring down the whole ministry in weeks.

When Amora saw that they were entering a church, her sense of doom heightened, and the voices in her head screamed in terror. It was always so much worse when a church was being "dedicated"—there was more bloodlust than usual, as the entities that were invoked seemed excessively more violent than at their temple.

That night, the church was filled with black-robed men and women, whose faces were shrouded in shadow because of the dim lighting. The air was thick with the smell of fear and evil as Amora was ushered to the front row seats just below the altar that had been set up on the stage. The whispered chanting of the priests and priestesses sent nervous chills up her back as she knew they were calling the dark ones to enter the room. Soon, the chants would put her into a trance-like state, where she could give little resistance to her part of the ritual.

A naked baby was the first to be placed on the white-clothed table, brought up and offered by its mother, a witch and breeder for the coven. Amora looked down at her feet, wanting to hide from the horrid scene, as the high priest, her father, sunk a blade into the crying baby's chest, soon silencing the child forever. The baby's blood was passed around in a chalice along with pieces of its flesh, and all ate and drank in a hellish communion to Satan. She was forced, as always, to partake of the vile elements. This is when her mind usually broke off, and something else would take over—but not that night. For some reason, her alter did not come up, and she was forced to fully engage in all emotions and experiences. Her youngest sister was brought up next, screaming and crying and laid on the altar for the first sex-magic ritual. Amora began to tremble and cry. Not wanting to witness what would be done, she began to back away. She backed into something and turned to see a large man with a long, black beard and black eyes; he smiled at her wickedly. His thick stonelike fist struck her hard in the face.

She woke up, naked, on the altar, terrified and in pain. As many of the men and women took their turns abusing her, she faded in and out of consciousness. She wished she would die, so it would end forever, and something inside her cried out to anyone in the universe who could hear or care to save her.

Suddenly, a bright light shone over her, and Amora no longer saw anyone or felt what was going on around her. The light was beautiful, like nothing she had ever seen before, as she felt it envelop all her senses. Amora smelled the scent of love, like rose and lavender, tasted acceptance like honey, and peace that covered her like a warm blanket inside and outside. As Amora reached up to touch the light, she began to rise out of her body and floated just above it. She looked around and, suddenly, a bright figure walked through the wall behind the altar into the sanctuary.

She heard a hellish scream, and a dark, thick, cloudy mist lifted off the coven and retreated quaking into a corner of the room away from the light. The bearded man of light had stunning eyes, the color of a clear summer sky. He smiled lovingly at her, and His voice came into her being.

"Amora, I am Jesus. You will live and not die. Satan fears your destiny. Worry not, for I will come for you, my precious daughter."

As He spoke, her chest felt as though it was a cup filling up and pouring over. She had never felt anything like it in her life. He held her gaze for a moment more, then turned and walked back through the wall, taking the light with Him. She tried to follow, but she could not move from her position floating above her body. She called, "Jesus! Come back! Jesus, please!"

Instantly, Amora was back in her body and sat up. "Jesus! Come back!"

A gasp erupted from the men and women around her, along with hisses and snarls.

"What did you say, girl?!" demanded her father.

She stammered, "I...uh..."

He yanked her off the altar by her arm and put his face in hers. "What did you see?!"

"I...nothing."

He shook her violently. "Don't lie to me!"

"He said his name was Jesus . . ." More hisses erupted from the coven.

He threw her on the ground. "That name is a curse . . . and you are guilty of betraying the coven! Betrayal equals death."

"What? But...but--"

He looked at a woman nearby. "Put her in the cage!"

They grabbed her, threw her robe in her arms, and abruptly and painfully marched her out. She was put in the back of a van with no windows and taken for a long ride. She thought of nothing but her experience with Jesus the whole way. She was nervous and afraid, but she remembered He said, "You will live and not die."

No matter what her father said, this man of light said that she wouldn't die. She decided to believe Him.

Amora was put in a large, dark cell filled with children in shackles. Chains were clamped on her ankles, and she was placed next to a little boy, who at first, she thought was asleep, but soon realized he was actually dead. Most of the other children stayed silent until someone came in to take one out. That child would scream and cry, everyone else would cover their ears and head and shiver, and the child never returned. Amora figured out that these were the children who were taken into the coven meetings for "sport," usually the first round of rape, torture, and murder, then thrown out like trash. At times, she had wondered where they came from but tried not to think too much about anything she saw and experienced in the meetings.

She didn't know how long she was there; there was no way to count days as there were no windows. Sometimes, they were brought water and bread, and it was then that she could see some of the children when light would be brought in. None of the keepers talked to them. The children were let out once a day to use the toilet, but it was so infrequent that most of them relieved themselves in the cage where they were kept. The smell sickened Amora for a time, but after some days, she became mostly nose blind to it.

When the dead boy next to her was finally removed, she saw that he was just skin and bones. She wondered if she would die here like him and sat with that dark thought for a while, until a quiet voice in her heart reminded her, *"You will live and not die."* She remembered the man called Jesus again and felt strengthened.

Eventually, Amora built up the courage to talk to the other children and was able to get some of them to speak to her. Many of them were from different parts of the world. Amora could understand the ones who spoke English, French, and German, but others spoke languages she could not understand. These children were orphans and street children in their native countries, so, sadly, no one would notice or care that they disappeared. The more Amora learned, the more she felt a desire to help these children.

During her time in the cage, Amora witnessed five children get taken out and never return, and she cried, knowing that torture and death awaited them. After what seemed like many days, they came for her. She fully expected to be taken to slaughter, but, surprisingly, she was showered and put in the small room instead. Still, no one said a word to her. A couple days passed and, occasionally, she heard voices outside her room. Her thoughts continually returned to her vision of Jesus. She wondered again if He was really going to come for her, and if He did, would He help the others too?

CHAPTER 16

Back in the cave of worlds, Gianna and Lucy had successfully translated from inside the cave to the top of Mount Joy three times and were feeling pretty good about themselves.

"Okay, ladies, that was great." The colors from the cave waters cascaded over Uriel's silvery-white hair, changing the hue intermittently. He explained, "This last training will let me know you are truly ready. Are both of you familiar with Cinderella's Castle at Disney World?"

Lucy jumped up and down and clapped, "Yes!"

Gianna nodded and elbowed Lucy.

"Good, now picture the castle and the stage in front of it. I want you to translate there."

"Uriel, not only is that farther away than what we've done, it's in another dimension," scoffed Gianna.

"Gianna, you must remove your limits." Uriel looked at her intently, but with a kindness that stirred Gianna. She could see he really cared about them and genuinely wanted them to succeed. "There are no time, space, or distance limits in the spirit! Those limitations are only in your mind!

If you can translate from the cave to the mountaintop, you can translate to Orlando, Florida, Timbuktu, or Mars!"

The girls looked at each other with wide eyes.

Lucy started bouncing again, "Let's try it!"

"Remember your focus. Now, picture the castle."

They nodded.

Gianna pictured the castle, then the stage, then being there with Lucy . . . and Yeshua was also standing there, holding Lucy's hand and pointing to different things in the park. She loved seeing the look of childlike excitement on Lucy's face. All of a sudden, she felt a familiar tingling in her legs, then through her arms, and suddenly there were the familiar blue spires.

The courtyard held a mass of people, young and old, and large cartoon characters and princesses stopping to hug and talk to children. There, right in front of her, were Lucy and Jesus holding hands, grinning wide at all the fun sights in the most magical place on earth.

David assembled the team in the cave of worlds, the light and color-filled waters making the walls seem alive with varied hues and textures. The team of angels and heroes stood solemn and statue-like around the kingly leader as he looked at each of them, the colors of the cave moving like a giant kaleidoscope across their varied, stoic faces.

The former king and military leader's visage was earnest, but his light brown eyes danced with joy. Gianna could see how the women of Israel could sing about his greatness. Getting to know David more over the last couple of days had brought it to another level. He was not only handsome but incredibly intelligent and kind. At times, she had to pinch herself to make sure this was real: angel warriors, gryphons, dragons, and Noah? This was not the cartoonish animal hugger from her son's coloring book!

David began to speak, and it snapped her back from her miscellaneous thoughts. "Today, we turn the tide of evil in this hour in history."

Gianna's stomach flipped nervously, and she began slow breathing as she focused on David's words.

"In ages past and present, great darkness has tried and failed, numerous times, to take over the earth realm. The enemy cannot seem to learn from his failures that he is doomed." David smiled while putting his arm around Lucy's shoulder. "Remember, our Champion has already won the victory! Lucifer is a loser destined for eternal punishment." He caught Gianna's eye. "Today, we will remind him of that fact by destroying his plans that were exposed by the spotlight of heaven!"

The group clapped and cheered.

"Okay, everyone, just a short reminder of our objectives. Team number one?" Uriel, Gianna, and Lucy nodded at him. "Save the young girl, Amora, heir to the Satanic Eastern Region. She is now the daughter of the True King, and with her, we will thwart even more plans of the evil one. Team number two?" Haniel, Lincoln, and Diego nodded. David continued, "You will turn the monster, Leviathan, against the false gods and wreck their planned destruction of island and seafaring habitations. Team number three?" Noah, Darrel, Billie Jean, Raphael, and Raguel nodded at David. "My team will keep the enemy invaders from getting through the portals until they close back up, locking the enemy's destroyers out of earth realm until the appointed time."

David was silent for a moment, looking at each human team member: Diego, Darrel, Lincoln, Gianna, Lucy, and Billie Jean. "I'm honored, as one of the Great Cloud of witnesses, to aid you in this endeavor."

"And I as well!" Noah bellowed as he clapped Darrel and Lincoln on the back. And they stumbled forward laughing.

The four angelic warriors, eyes shining, nodded in agreement with Noah and David's words. Striking their spears and swords to the ground in beat, they began to chant in a heavenly tongue what sounded like a musical military cadence.

Diego and the team didn't understand the chant but felt strength rise up inside.

Noah translated:

"We go with the might of heaven!

We go with the Holy!

We go with the Right Arm of the Almighty!

We go with the Lamb and with His Bride!"

David led them in prayer, and when finished, simply stated, "It's time."

The Prince of Darkness stood brooding on top of Mount Woe, his coal-black eyes gazing out over the legions of giants, monsters, and the myriad of other dark-realm creatures created and conjured up for this day of doom.

Calculating hundreds of moves ahead, his ancient mind, without need of sleep or nutrients, far surpassed an earthly grandmaster chess player. For thousands of years, he had studied his Enemy and His pathetic human offspring. He constantly stopped himself from breaking forth into undignified chuckles. No, not yet. Not until he witnessed the terror of thousands of screaming human faces as his children poured through the portals to destroy and devour everything they came upon. He tapped his fingers together with delight and allowed himself a slight grin as he thought of it.

Oh, but there was one thing that still gnawed at his thoughts and kept him slightly unsettled—the possibility of the Son of Man thwarting his schemes. Frowning at the prospect, his pacing became more agitated and impatient as he thought of the humans at Mount Joy. He was no fool to think that YHWH would sit back and watch while he destroyed the precious "image-bearers." Lucifer spit with revulsion as his hatred boiled up again for the nasty "mud-men," as he liked to call them. He still chuckled at the foolishness of making a being from dirt and then putting divinity in it! *Repulsive!*

"BAAL!" He roared.

The massive principality appeared before Satan and bowed. "Yes, my Master."

"Has the stealth team reported back yet? We are literally at the brink of beginning!"

Baal hesitated.

"WHAT IS THE PROBLEM?!"

"There has been no word from them, Master. . . nothing."

"Has there been anyone sent to check on them?"

"Yes, master, and there's no sign of them, there is fear that they've been . . . captured."

Satan closed his eyes to contain the absolute rage and hate that was on the edge of bursting. He knew there was only one being capable of capturing his stealth team, and that would be Michael himself. He HATED him. He clenched his fists, shaking with anger and muttering Michael's name, along with a varied array of profanities under his breath. He would have his day of vengeance on the Prince of Israel. *Soon.*

"No matter." He cracked his neck, and his face was again devoid of emotion. "We're too far to let this hinder us now. They can't stop us all; we're too numerous and heading to too many parts of the earth. Tell the human servants to begin the portal rituals; the stars are aligned almost perfectly now."

Baal bowed. "Yes, Master."

CHAPTER 17

Uriel, Gianna, and Lucy arrived in the middle of a field. The full moon was bright overhead and shined down on them like a spotlight. It was cold.

"Follow me, there's no time to waste. We must quickly get to Amora before they move her to the area of sacrifice," Uriel whispered urgently.

The girls nodded and followed, hearts pumping with fear and adrenaline. Gianna estimated they had traveled about half a mile before they arrived at a wall made of thick stone that stretched for miles to the left and right and rose at least 12 feet above their heads. The section they stood in front of was lined with vines and surrounded by thick trees.

"What's behind this wall?" asked Lucy.

"A castle where the children are being held. It will be easier to get Amora from here than when she's moved to a heavily fortified facility closer to Cern. We literally have minutes before they get her. I'm going to distract and take care of the guards. I need you both to put your skills to work now; go to her cell and translate her out."

"But...but how do we do that when we've not seen the room before? When we practiced, we could picture where we were going." Gianna was getting more nervous with the expectation of performing what they had learned.

"Don't worry," he answered. "It's the same; just picture Amora and set your will and desire to go to her."

"But...I don't know what she looks like!" Lucy whispered frantically.

"Shhhh...okay, just relax, breathe in and out slowly."

Gianna and Lucy both took some deep breaths.

"Okay, good. Both of you close your eyes. Good. Listen to my voice and concentrate. Get a picture of Amora in your head, whatever you think she looks like is fine. She's 11 years old, blonde hair, blue eyes, alone in a small room with just a cot. Can you see that?"

They nodded.

"Okay. Now...go to her."

The girls disappeared. Uriel transformed into his spirit form and walked through the wall.

Amora, worried about her sisters, had just finished a

prayer to the Man of Light. The hours she had spent in the small room gave her too much time to think. She wondered what would happen to Anna and Alanna if she died. She also worried for the other children kept prisoner in this castle. Suddenly, a wind blew through her room, and two ladies appeared in her cell. She rubbed her eyes in disbelief.

They stared at her and looked just as surprised as she was. They were dressed in dark clothes and cloaks. One looked like a teenager, and not much bigger than herself, and the other was a beautiful woman, with muscled arms and a kind face. Her mouth dropped as she recognized the woman from her dream. Even though some of her dreams and visions had come true in the past, it still startled her when it happened. The lady whispered, "Amora?"

"H-How do you know my name? Did Jesus send you?"

The lady blinked in surprise. "Yes! Do you know Him?"

"He told me I wouldn't die, and He would save me! Are you going to take me to Him?"

The lady smiled nervously. "We're going to get you out of here and to a safe place. You will have to trust us, okay?"

Amora nodded.

The teenager whispered, "Do you have shoes and a coat?"

Amora shook her head, "Only what I have on."

The ladies looked worried. She was wearing only a thin nightgown. The woman took her cloak off and draped it over Amora's shoulders.

"I'm Gianna, and this is Lucy. Don't worry, okay?"

Amora nodded again.

"Okay, great. Come on, we need to leave quickly. Just hold our hands, and we're going to take you with us, the same way you saw us come in, okay?"

Gianna grabbed Amora's hand. Amora shook her head.

"Wait! I can't leave without them. The other children. Can you save them too?"

Gianna and Lucy looked at each other and frowned.

"No, sweetie, I'm sorry. I wish we could, but we can only get you out. We don't have much time left before they come for you."

"Please! You have to help them! They've got no one, and they're all going to die."

Gianna shushed her. "Look, we have little time, and we've got to keep you out of their hands to prevent the end of the world. So, please, just come with us quickly."

Amora looked at them and realized what they were talking about. She shook her head. "Saving me won't prevent what you're talking about. They have others lined up; they always have others. You've got to get us all out, and then you've got to take out my father. He's the one that knows all the spells and rituals!"

Now Lucy and Gianna were really worried. Just then, they heard a thump outside the door, and Gianna's heart dropped. She was about to forcefully grab the little girl's hand and leave when Uriel appeared in the room. He looked calm but urgent.

"Why are you still here? The guards were on their way in, and I took them out, but we've got to go; more will come."

They quickly explained the delay to Uriel, who nodded thoughtfully. "The girl is right."

"We didn't prepare for this, Uriel. We can't possibly rescue these kids."

"We must," he said simply.

Before she could argue, He put his arms around all three of them. They disappeared and reappeared in a dark room filled with several locked cages and possibly the worst smell Gianna had ever experienced. She coughed and covered her mouth and nose with her hand, as did Lucy and Amora.

"We have to work quickly," Uriel said, as the locks on all the cages fell open and dropped to the ground. "Listen carefully, ladies. You will grab 2 or 3 children each, and I will help you transport them to a place outside the wall. We must do this several times. Don't question; just start."

Uriel illuminated a wall near the back, providing enough light to see the cages and children. Gianna's stomach turned from the sight now, rather than the smell. Each pen held seven or eight kids of different ages, most naked, filthy, and skinny, all chained like animals.

"Gianna, don't look; just get them out. The chains are unlocked, tell them to take them off!" Uriel urged.

Gianna nodded and walked into the nearest cage. The children cried and cowered.

"Hey, it's okay, darlings; we're here to save you...I promise. You have to stand up now and take the chains off. Quickly, please, we have to leave now."

One or two children stood up and took the shackles off, but the others still sat cowering. Gianna went to them one by one and stood them up. Some were too feeble to stand, so she had the stronger ones help the weak. She put a toddler in the arms of a six or seven-year-old and grabbed another two, while a couple others followed her out. She met Uriel, who had six in tow, and Lucy, who had another five; Amora had three.

Uriel told the rest, "We'll be back quickly for the rest of you, stay quiet." He looked at Gianna and Lucy. "Everyone, hold on to one of us." He nodded, and they all disappeared. At once, they were outside the stone wall under cover of the trees. Uriel looked at Amora. "I need you to mind them while we go back in. Don't move and stay under cover of these trees."

She nodded. He took Gianna and Lucy's hands, and they vanished.

Back in the cells, the girls and Uriel gathered the rest of the children, many of whom were too weak to stand. Uriel managed to grab all the weak ones. As they exited the cages, the door to the room burst open, and guards dressed in black uniforms ran in shouting, "Stop!" while pointing guns in their direction.

Gianna began to panic. "Uriel?!"

Alarms were blaring, and the children began to cry.

"Do not fear! Grab onto me!" cried Uriel.

They vanished, just as the guards reached them.

Instantly, the team reappeared where they had left Amora and the others. They were surprised and relieved to find two other angel warriors with Amora and the rescued children. Uriel approached them.

"We must go quickly; did you find a safe place for the children?"

The dark-haired, fully armed angels nodded. "In Mozambique."

Alarms blared all around, and lights blazed from over the walls.

The two warriors scooped up a few weak children each, as did Uriel, Gianna, and Lucy. There were about thirty children altogether. They motioned for the others to grab onto them.

"Go!" said Uriel.

And with that, they vanished.

CHAPTER 18

Lincoln stood on his floating platform in the middle of the Pacific Ocean, holding an unfathomably light, yet deadly, spear in his hand, dressed in the most advanced wet-suit armor yet to be seen on the earth. The dark gray suits, equipped with a cloaking feature, covered their body, and the form-fitting helmets featured a full 360° view. The suit felt like a second skin. It regulated their body temperature and oxygen levels, protected their ears, and kept nitrogen at safe levels so they could dive deep at accelerated speeds.

Lincoln was enthralled with heaven tech, and pestered Haniel relentlessly to show him other incredible weapons they had "up there." Haniel placated him by promising to show him more when, *and only when,* they finished their task successfully!

After a while, Lincoln's thoughts began to drift away from the new suit onto inevitably mulling over his list of perceived failures. He found the "quiet time" on the platform gave him too much opportunity to contemplate his decisions up to that point in time. Trying to shake himself from the dark path of thought, he wandered into random reflection.

Did I let the dog out before I went to sleep the other night? I wonder if my kids miss me. I hope the Jets have a shot at the Super Bowl this year. Are there any big sharks in the water right now? I wish there were so that I could try this spear out!

He finally decided to sing to himself to keep his mind focused. Diego was many yards away on another platform, and the undulation of the waves made it so that Lincoln could only see the professor when a wave got underneath and lifted it up. Each time, Lincoln would holler and whistle until Diego reciprocated. It helped pass the time anyway, as he figured they'd been out there at least an hour waiting for Haniel's signal.

Apparently, they were positioned directly above the gate of Leviathan. Lincoln got a cold shiver when he thought about what they were about to do; tangle with a sea monster with the temperament of a wild boar that made Godzilla look like a puppy. Not to mention, the two gods they would attempt to kill in order to save the world. Lincoln still hoped sometimes that this was a dream, and he would wake up any second in his warm bed next to his wife.

Just then, Haniel popped out of the water between

them. "They've opened the gate! Turn on your spears and follow me!"

Lincoln sucked in his breath as his adrenaline spiked, and his heartbeat raced. He gripped his spear tight with anticipation, as he and Diego dove in the water and followed the angel into the depths.

Meanwhile, David's team arrived on Mount Woe, which appeared like an exact replica of Mount Joy. There was no difference between the mountains, as far as Darrel observed, except that this pinnacle was in a dark realm like a circle of Hell. Upon arrival, Darrel instantly felt squeezed from the inside out, which had caused an immediate panic attack. The atmosphere was thick with a hazy red-orange color; whatever was in the air made it hard to think and breathe. He and Billie Jean both began coughing and wheezing, each breath taking immense effort. Darrel fell to his knees, panic rising, as his vision blackened, and he felt a thousand pounds pressing on his chest.

Noah and David didn't seem affected, and they quickly sprang into action, placing their hands on him and Billie Jean. Suddenly, Darrel felt a power come out of them like liquid energy, completely covering his being. In moments, he and Billie Jean were on their feet and breathing normally.

"What came out of your hands? I feel invincible!" said Billie Jean.

Noah chuckled and hugged her close. "That, my dear girl, is called glory. Hundreds of years of worship at the throne of the King of the Universe comes with many benefits!"

They quickly split up, Noah and Billie Jean going to one area, David and Darrel heading to another where they could watch high above the evil hordes that waited below for the portals to open.

David and Darrel crouched low on a cliff overlooking the Nephilim armies, who stood in block formation. The enemy would soon discover their presence, so they had to act fast.

"This is the perfect moment to attack," Darrel whispered urgently. "They're all standing there together waiting to be shot."

"We can't lose the element of surprise."

David's calm demeanor perplexed Darrel.

"So, what are we waiting for? Let's go!"

Darrel, stirred with adrenaline and fear, wanted to go now before he lost his nerve.

"We've got to tarry for the signal, little brother."

David patted his shoulder reassuringly. "Raphael knows what he's doing here. The timing must be just right."

Lucifer and his generals had lost communication with his Stealth Team and were having no luck finding out what happened to them. Michael, himself, had the team under lock and key in his own dungeons and had done brilliantly getting them to spill much-needed intel. It would be ages before Lucifer would get word about their fate.

Meanwhile, Raphael and Raguel took the form of two of the elite team and were able to move through the enemy horde undetected. They soon found the troop of Baal's sons awaiting the opening of Abaddon's gate. The pair arrived just before Lucifer, and within moments, took out the whole troop before any of the Nephilim detected the angels' presence. It was a full-on slaughter, faster than lightning, as more than forty were down before the others even realized what was happening. By the time Lucifer arrived, to find a pile of dead and decapitated giants, the two angels had slipped far away.

The dark prince seethed in rage as he scanned the dead, with Baal aghast and trembling by his side.

How could this happen without even an inkling of detection!?

"SOUND THE ALARM! THEY'RE HERE AMONG US! CHECK EVERY CREATURE!!" Lucifer thundered.

Below David and Darrel, the throngs of enemy creatures who had once stood at attention began to scatter in multiple directions. In a flash, Raphael flew up into the sky above the mountain top and blew a golden shofar. The deep sound reverberated off the cliff walls and into the dank atmosphere. Darrel felt the vibration go through him, and his spirit leaped in response. Immediately, gleaming angelic warriors swarmed in from every direction.

Darrel looked wide-eyed at David. "Where were they? Why didn't you tell us?"

David smiled and held up his hands, "Surprise!!"

"How many?"

"About 100, they came at the last minute. They didn't want to miss the action!" David began to run towards the edge of the mountain. "Let's go! That was the signal!"

David leaped off the mountain, sword in hand, and like a skydiver glided towards the ground below. Noah's loud battle cry soon followed, and the patriarchs landed side by side like a couple of cats leaping off a table. Darrel, his whole body aflame, jumped off the mountain, flying directly into the fray of sword clashing angels and flying monsters.

His momentary fear of flight and battle quickly turned to thrill, and Darrel began to laugh with excitement as he zoomed into the thick of it. His flames took down dozens of giant bats, harpies, and hellish flying gargoyles. Immediately, Billie Jean, in her gryphon form, joined him as she expertly tore apart everything in her path. Darrel shook his head and smiled. "What a woman!"

Seeing the angelic army arrive, Lucifer cursed under his breath. Undaunted, he clenched his fists and turned to Baal.

"AS SOON AS THE PORTALS OPEN, GO! DO NOT LET ANYTHING STOP OUR TROOPS FROM ENTERING THOSE GATES!"

Baal bowed and left quickly to update the generals.

One by one, large circular openings began to appear, some along the ground and some opening up in the middle of the milky-red sky. As each portal opened, ten or so angelic warriors surrounded it to cut down various monstrosities that attempted to get through.

Billie Jean let out a shriek that shook the mountain and scattered dark flying creatures left and right, many grabbing their ears in pain. In earnest, she took out any flying thing that came near a portal. Darrel, a blazing ball of fiery destruction, aimed for nearby gateways, and took out gargoyles, gremlins, and screechers who attempted to get through.

His fire balls and flame streams were particularly effective against nasty hybrids of centaurs and satyrs, who were not the beautiful, gentle creatures of childhood stories. These were true monsters, who lived only for murder and terror. If he hadn't been so busy blasting them, fear would have crippled Darrel at the sight of these living nightmares. However, he did ponder the horror they would bring on earth to innocent people if they happened to get through a portal. To make sure that didn't happen, Darrel fought even harder.

The Waking

On the ground, David and Noah fought side-by-side with sword and axe, a formidable and deadly duo, going toe to toe with ten to twenty-foot giants, and bringing them down in piles. The putrid smell of the titans was nauseating, and David remarked, "We probably should've warned the team about the rank stench of Nephilim! Ack! Haven't smelled this kind of reek in millennia. It may knock poor Darrel to the ground!"

Noah, having just wrested his axe from the corpse of a 12-foot berserker, shrugged. "Eh, you get used to it after a bit, brother! Quit your whining and bring down that tiny one coming in behind ya'!"

David turned in time to dodge the club of a skyscraper-sized, ginger-bearded howler with fangs the size of David's sword. Noah laughed, enjoying every bit of the adrenaline rush of the fight. "Come at me, you cursed pile of dung!"

The giant ran towards them, and Noah and David jumped up, quickly slicing through both hamstrings like a choreographed dance, and bringing the brute to the ground with a thunderous howl. In a flash, Noah sliced its fighting arm clean off while David decapitated it mid-howl.

Raphael and Raguel, still hidden among the dark ranks,

took out whole troops of Nephilim in minutes. Soon though, many giants re-assessed and began to scatter into teams. They started to evade the duo's lethal swords and hunt their attackers. The two angels finally gave up the ruse and transformed into their true forms, confronting giants and trolls head to head, significantly slowing down their kill count.

Even while it seemed their team had the upper hand of power and surprise, Darrel noticed they would soon be overcome by sheer numbers. As far as his eyes could see, more and more horrible hordes slowly moved forward. He wondered how long they could successfully keep them from getting through the portals, and how much longer it would be before they closed.

Meanwhile, Lincoln and Diego followed Haniel down to the depths of The Devil's Triangle.

"I'm too old for this," Diego thought as he swam closer to a fiery ocean floor crack easily the size of New Jersey.

Standing on the edge of the fissure were two hulking figures, each holding a golden trident. They recognized one of them as Dagon, the four-armed fish god. The other, larger being, stood on gigantic squid-like tentacles instead of legs, his long hair moving slowly behind him in the water.

That must be Oceanus. Diego chuckled nervously. *I'll let Lincoln tangle with that one.*

Fear not, my son, I am with you. The Comforter's voice quietly dropped into his thoughts.

Diego relaxed a bit. *My Lord! Yes! I remember.*

Haniel held his hand up and stopped them a few yards away. He pointed to his eyes, then at the figures. Diego and Lincoln nodded. The men watched the glowing fissure. Diego felt a dark, icy shadow wrap around his spirit, and he shivered, just before he saw the darkness ascend and block out the light from the crevice.

Then multiple, clawed tentacles began to emerge from the crack, penetrating deep into the surrounding rock. The two gods moved back. Even from that distance, Diego could tell that fear had gripped them. Soon, the dragon-like head of the ancient sea monster emerged over the crag, with sword-like teeth and searching red-serpentine eyes. Diego's heart filled with terror and awe as he saw this primordial beast emerge from thousands of years of captivity. The creature's eyes disclosed that the ancient being was not a mindless monster but an entity of vast intelligence. It quickly spotted the gods, who at that moment ignited their tridents. Instantly, the beast locked onto them like a bull to a torero, and both gods hurried towards the surface.

Lincoln and Diego sprang into action and threw their lighted spears, each landing true through the entities' chests, whose eyes became circles of surprise. Haniel came quickly behind and, with ease, pinned Dagon to the ocean floor. Oceanus recovered in seconds and began to swim, torpedo-like, knowing his life was in peril. Haniel followed in close pursuit.

Diego and Lincoln watched as the great beast descended on Dagon, whose scream rang clear through the deep, calling to attention many fish and sharks, which began to swim in his direction. What use could they be against the primeval monster? Leviathan devoured Dagon in one bite, and to Lincoln's delight, left behind the spear!

Sufficiently cloaked by their suits, Diego and Lincoln seemed relatively safe from Leviathan's detection for the time being. The giant beast jetted past them in fast pursuit of Oceanus' light. Diego was again astounded at the size of the monster and wondered if it would be able to see them even if they weren't cloaked, as their relative size to it were as ants to humans!

The Waking

Lincoln retrieved the spear, and they followed the beast, wondering how they would assist Haniel in the next stage of this great endeavor.

Billie Jean's view from the sky gave her a superior advantage in watching the enemy's movements. Their first surge seemed to be a mad scramble towards the gates, which was met and squelched swiftly by the team and angelic warriors. She went to work enthusiastically, attacking anything that came her way. She enjoyed the powerful gryphon's body and the looks of terror it brought to the villains' faces as she ripped them to shreds with her massive talons and beak. She and the heavenly host seemed to be doing well at keeping back harpies, flying serpents, and other large monsters. The harder ones to spot and stop were the tiny, but deadly, fairies, flying gremlins, and gnomes. Billie Jean wasn't sure if a few small, sneaky things were making it through, especially on the ground where the team was more focused on the giants. She was getting as many as she saw with her sharp eagle eyes, both on and off the ground.

Billie Jean soon spotted David and Noah directly below, doing significant damage to the ground armies. She was amazed at the speed in which the fierce pair were bringing the formidable giants down. Soon, though, it became apparent that the enemy numbers continued to surge. They seemed to be rethinking their initial strategy of randomly rushing the gates. Now, they were regathering and moving forward in great solid walls, so that even though many were taken out, the sheer numbers allowed quite a few to make it to the portals and slip through.

The raven-haired captain of the 100 heavenly warriors began to disperse some of his troops to help on the ground. He nodded to Billie Jean, and she understood that she was being asked to step up her game. She nodded back and began more offensive attacks. She effectively dive-bombed the horde, scooping up larger goblin warriors and dropping them on top of others from great heights. She soon caught a brief glimpse of Darrel as he flew like a comet towards an immense group of short, stocky trolls, lighting the whole company ablaze.

David and Noah backed up as a two-headed, thirty-foot, smelly monstrosity attempted to crush them beneath its six-toed, house-sized feet. Their supernatural speed kept them out of harm's way and succeeded in making the much slower giant exceedingly angry.

Noah elbowed David. "Let's have some fun and see if we can get both heads working against each other before we relieve them of their necks."

David guffawed loudly as he dodged a tree-sized club from the giant. They ran in different directions through the monster's legs, slicing its ankles along the way. Its furious screams from both mouths shook the ground as it strained to look in two directions simultaneously. In short order, it lost its balance and fell gloriously on top of dozens of nasty beasts below it that were too slow to get out of the way. The two biblical heroes whooped joyously and immediately went in for the kill. They soon had both massive, ugly heads cleanly severed from the titan's enormous, smelly body.

"Gah! If that's not the ugliest thing I've seen in 5000 years . . . who could have been the father of this disgusting thing?!" Noah spat as he got a close look at one of the severed heads.

"Be careful what you wish for, brother! Let's hope we don't meet the progenitor of this one, eh?" quipped David.

Their conversation was soon cut short as they heard a rumble behind them and turned to see a vast throng, at least a thousand strong, of mythic beasts heading straight at them. The men quickly squared up, realizing they were all that stood between those murderous entities and the portal. Noah raised a shofar to his lips and blew.

CHAPTER 19

Gianna, Lucy, and Uriel suddenly appeared at David and Noah's side as an army of giants and monsters rushed toward them. Wide-eyed, they sprang into action. Lucy raised an invisible wall that the first row of monsters slammed into. They fell and began to pile up in a great heap while the other beasts climbed over the unfortunate first row, fighting to get through and over them...

"What just happened?" Gianna gasped as she felt the power rush begin in her arms.

Uriel answered simply, "Noah's shofar can create a portal. We were pulled through it."

Noah whooped with excitement at seeing them. He patted Lucy. "How long can you hold that shield, little lady?"

Lucy, sweating profusely, answered, "I really don't know. This is, like, the first time I've ever tried this. So, think of something quick, okay!?"

Noah winked at her. "No worries, little sister. Uriel and I have been in worse predicaments and prevailed. Right, brother?"

Uriel slapped Noah on the back, causing the jolly man to stumble forward. "Remember our battle with the sons of Semyaza?"

Noah, regaining his footing, laughed. "How can I forget?! Nasty, ugly beasts with four arms, some of them, eh?"

David raised an eyebrow, "Let's reminisce later, brothers, okay? We have work to do!"

"Wait 'til you see what we have in our back pocket!" Shouted Noah. "That Semyaza battle happened to turn the tide of the Nephil tyranny in that area! Where are Raphael and Raquel? We need them!"

As if they were waiting for their names to be called, the two stealth warriors appeared at the team's side.

"I hear tell we're needed for giant bashin'!?" Raguel yelled as he punched his hand.

Uriel winked at Raguel and Raphael. "I think it's time to turn the tide, brothers!"

They stood side by side like a glorious, angelic wall in front of the human warriors.

Uriel yelled, "Lucy, take your shield down! All of you stand back!"

The three heavenly warriors linked arms and began to

radiate light. Lucy gladly released her shield, and she and the others backed up, covering their eyes. Suddenly, a wave of holy, atomic power blasted forth from the angels, immediately disintegrating the massive enemy horde in front of them.

On top of Mount Woe, Lucifer screamed in rage as he watched a third of his army wiped out by the three angels in the valley below. Nevertheless, he had calculated a contingency plan in case the *Enemy* thwarted him. He needed a distraction.

"TAKE THEM OUT!" He roared at Baal.

The bull-headed god nodded and jumped off the mountain. His landing shook the ground, sending rock and sand exploding in all directions. His already massive ten-foot frame began to grow and expand, his horns lengthened and curled behind. In horrible circular rings, his eyes turned to flames as he lifted his head and roared a deep, dark sound that caused the humans' stomachs to drop and arm hairs to raise. Skeletal black spider-like appendages burst from his waist, lifting him off the ground, carrying him swiftly towards them. Behind him, two enormous dragons landed and lumbered forward—one onyx-black, and one a mesmerizing opalescent color.

"Spread out and attack!" commanded Uriel.

Billie Jean and Darrel quickly flew over to aid when they saw the dark god descend to attack their friends.

Raphael and Raguel took off into the air, giant swords blazing, each going after a dragon, as Noah and David ran the ground attack underneath them. Uriel took a stand in front of Baal, with his massive sword drawn and glowing. Darrel, like a flaming missile, shot towards the dark god who easily swatted him out of the sky. He landed hard several yards away, forming a deep crater. Billie Jean flapped above Baal's head and let out a gryphon call, causing the god to double over and cover his ears. He recovered abruptly, taking her by surprise when a few of his nasty appendages struck out towards her, one slicing her left side before she could react. She flew to a safer distance, wounds stinging and throbbing. Uriel took advantage of the distraction and spun like a deadly tornado of light, slicing through two legs from the top, causing the dark god to crash face-first into the ground.

Meanwhile, Gianna and Lucy were about to join in against the dragons when they realized there were creatures, including some decent-sized giants, making it through a few portals. Even though the heavenly hosts were bringing down vast numbers of monsters at specific points, other areas seemed to lack manpower, causing a breach. Gianna didn't want to consider what was happening on the other side of those gates on earth.

"Lucy!" Gianna called. "Take that gate on the upper right, and I'll take the one further down and see if we can help close it off!"

Lucy nodded and flew off.

At the portal, Gianna made quick work of slicing through a pack of hideous gargoyles and a pair of vicious goat-men. More and more nightmare creatures came towards her, and without fear, she cut through them. It fueled her by knowing how awful it would be if they made it through to attack innocent men, women, and children on the other side.

A massive minotaur thundered towards her, and she barely escaped a goring. The bull-man was a fierce beast to bring down. It relentlessly moved forward, even after she had stabbed it multiple times. Fortunately, with a powerful sweep of its legs, she plunged a blade through its eye seconds before it got to the portal. Meanwhile, at least a dozen monsters got through—including a few gnomes, complete with red pointed hats, a pair of leprechauns, and a terrifying werewolf. Gianna screamed in frustration and kicked a small gremlin, sending it screaming across the bloody valley. This was like sticking a finger in a leaking dam ready to break! As she continued fighting, her anger and frustration at the futility of what they were doing mounted. Finally, she thought to pray.

Father, we need you! They're getting through! Please! How do we close the gates?

The gentle whisper answered. *Daughter, blood for blood. They spilled innocent blood to open the gates. There must be repentance and forgiveness rendered to close them.*

She stood still, having just finished off a pig-shaped beast.

Can I do that?

Everything around her went silent as if someone pushed a pause button on a video.

I give you authority over the power of the enemy. Whatever you bind on earth will be bound in heaven; whatever you forgive will be forgiven.

The dragons saw that Baal was down, and they promptly left fighting the angels to defend their master. The giant reptiles immediately began to stir up a whirlwind of rock and sand with their massive wings while spewing fire in every direction. The team spread out and moved far from the fray to avoid getting fried and pummeled.

Baal was then able to recover; his spider legs pulled back into his body. He stood ready to fight again as the fire and rock storm began to die down. From between the two flying beasts, he grinned wickedly at the team and goaded them to come at him.

Lucifer watched the tumult from his perch on top of Mount Woe. Satisfied that his Enemy's teams were sufficiently distracted, he called his private guards to send word to initiate the final contingency plan. They bowed, but as they turned to obey, their heads fell from their bodies, and Satan had a sword at his throat before he had time to react.

"I see you were sent to clean up the mess, as usual . . . *brother.*" Lucifer emphasized the last word with an eye-roll.

"Your proficiency at creating them has made me an expert at it...*brother.*" Michael spat to the side as he said the last word.

"What will you do, Michael? You know it's not yet time to shackle me?!"

"Yah, rebuke you, Lucifer! It may not be time to shackle you yet, but a little punishment and humiliation will do just fine for now!" He touched his sword tip to Lucifer's neck. "Draw ...your... sword!"

Satan back-flipped onto a high rock face, black sword drawn. "With pleasure, *brother!*"

Michael removed his tunic and cracked his neck twice, his muscles pulsing with anticipation. His long, raven hair was tied back similarly to the dark prince, but his resemblant coal-black eyes sparkled with glory light rather than death. He had been anticipating this reunion, predicting the exact moment he would, yet again, help forestall his wayward brother's nefarious schemes.

They flew at each other, and their swords clashed with a thunderous crack. For a brief moment, the fighting below them paused. Then, just as quickly, the fighting resumed.

Satan parried and flipped like an expert gymnast, avoiding the power of Michael's slashes by a hair's breadth. The angel's movements were so fast that any human watching would only have seen flashes of light and heard clangs of metal as the swords struck each other.

Suddenly, Michael's sword caught the top of Satan's right arm in mid-spin, which threw his momentum, allowing the heavenly prince to land a fist to his enemy and brother's face. Lucifer fell, and Michael slashed down as Lucifer rolled, avoiding four lightning-quick stabs. In a flash, he round-house kicked Michael's legs, bringing the heavenly prince down for a moment while Lucifer dodged his counter-kick and sword slice.

Like a cat, the dark prince sprang over him, rolled into a somersault, popped up and turned, slashing downward with his black blade. Michael parried and landed another hard fist-crack to Satan's face, causing the snake to stumble back wide-eyed.

Speedily, Michael kicked him hard into the rock wall, producing an indention and sending stone shards flying. The impact caused Lucifer to drop his sword. Michael rushed forward with his blade, but in a flash, the dark prince moved, and round-house kicked it from Michael's hand. Soon, they were trading blows, Michael landing many quick and short, and Lucifer landing a few hard and powerful until Michael got his brother to the ground in a grappling move that rendered him powerless to budge for a time. Lucifer stubbornly refused to yield.

Down below in the valley, Gianna took a deep breath, her heart beating noisily in her ears. She looked at the battlefield, her friends, worn out and bloody, but still fighting courageously against the hordes of monsters on every side. Could she really stop this? Immediately, all the impossible scenarios she had witnessed the past few days flashed across the movie screen of Gianna's mind until the last picture—Yeshua looking at her from the cross with eyes of pure love. A single tear slipped down her cheek, and she prayed, "Father, I repent for the innocent blood spilled for evil this day! I ask that you cover the sin with the blood of the Savior, forgive it, and nullify the power of the effects of that sin! I bind the agents of evil that even now are perpetrating heinous acts of violence against your children! I forbid the enemy from passing through and ask that you close the gates!"

Thunder boomed. The ground shook as multitudes of lightning bolts illuminated the sky. A collective wail resounded from the Devil's hordes. Wherever a lightning bolt hit, the ground began to split, and dozens of demonic creatures fell into the darkness below. Then a voice resounded across the macabre land, "YOUR PRAYERS ARE ANSWERED, DAUGHTER."

Suddenly, a shofar sounded from the portal directly behind Uriel and others. Baal's eyes instantly went from fiery defiance to terror-filled. The angels looked up just as Haniel flew through the opening and over their heads, followed by the massive monster, Leviathan.

Lincoln and Diego, riding on top of the ancient beast, threw their red-glowing spears directly into the center of Baal's chest. The ancient monster immediately swallowed him whole. Both dragons attempted to flee but were devoured like mice being eaten by a lion. The portal that the heroes had come through instantly closed, with all other portals shutting right after.

Hearing the shofar from the top of Mount Woe, Michael loosened his grip, allowing Lucifer to pop up just in time to see Leviathan devour Baal and the dragons.

If Satan were capable of producing tears, Michael might have seen some that day. Instead, he lifted his head and screamed in a rage so deep it caused Michael to take a knee. He turned to Michael. "I wouldn't let your guard down just yet, brother. I would be a fool to have only one plan in play."

Michael fixed his dark gaze on his brother and gave a slight nod.

Lucifer turned his eyes back to the fray below. "Until we meet again, brother!" He transformed into a pearlescent, ebony dragon, and flew into the red sky, away from his minions in peril below.

CHAPTER 20

On the battlefield, the teams and heavenly host wisely moved from the path of the great beast; Lucy covered herself and the humans nearby with a protective forcefield. They all watched, open-mouthed, as Leviathan made quick work of eating every monster, giant, and fiend in its path. Haniel grabbed Diego and Lincoln from the beast's back and flew them to Michael's side atop Mount Woe. The other angels and heroes followed close behind. Yeshua soon appeared in the midst of them, and they all bowed low. He was dressed regally in white and gold robes, the glory of His presence lighting up the dark of the area around them. They all noticed they could breathe easier in His presence.

"Arise, mighty warriors."

As they stood, He looked at each of them with tenderness and pride. Diego and Lincoln still dressed in sleek gray water suits, and next to them, Darrel, covered in a layer of rock dust, spattered with blood. Beside him stood Billie Jean, in her human form, seemingly unfazed by the bloody gash across her belly. Lucy, with her torn cloak and black monster goo spattering her face, grinned widely. He raised his hands and blessed them. Gianna's emotions swept in, and she hung her head.

He approached and gently lifted her chin. "Sweet daughter, I know you feel you've failed me, but I assure you that is not the case."

"But, Master, if I had thought to pray sooner, so many of them wouldn't have gotten through."

He shook His head. "You miss the fact that you did pray, and you closed the gates, daughter."

He turned to the others. "All of you defeated the plan of the Wicked One! You caused such devastation to the enemy this day that he won't recover for ages! Rejoice!"

The heavenly host instantly shouted and clapped, and many blew shofars. It took the heroes a moment to catch up, as they were exhausted, shocked, and overwhelmed, but soon they couldn't help but join in. Within minutes, the claps of joy turned into praise to the Lamb. His glory fell on them like a thick cloud, and soon the outward expression moved to diving deeply into His love, which invaded every cell and atom in their beings.

Gianna laid on the ground, prostrate at His feet, wanting to do nothing else but adore Him. She could no longer see anyone around her but Him; no care, worry, or fear entered her mind, nor was she capable of anything but love and adoration. She completely surrendered her being to worship.

After some time, possibly hours or months—no one could comprehend how much time had passed—the cloud slowly thinned and disappeared. One by one, they stood up and realized they were back in the cave of worlds. The hundreds of heavenly warriors were gone; only Yeshua remained, dressed again as a humble traveler, and the original team, along with their new friends: David, Noah, Uriel, Haniel, Raphael, and Raguel.

David addressed the team, his eyes watering with emotion. "It was such a pleasure to serve with you, mighty warriors! I'm saddened that our time has come to an end and that we have to say goodbye."

He bear-hugged each of them.

Noah began to embrace the team as well and, at the end, approached Lincoln and Diego, shaking his head and grinning. "You lot blew my mind! Riding Leviathan in like a rodeo bull and saving the day; the rocks you must have!" He picked them up and squeezed them together, causing them both to grunt loudly. "Call me anytime you need an extra sword for a fight!"

After saying their last goodbyes, David and Noah

walked through a glowing, yellow water portal and were gone. The six unlikely heroes looked to the Master for instruction.

"It's time for you all to go home. You will wake up the morning after you first fell asleep. However, the world has indeed changed. Overnight many creatures breached the gates and have physically manifested in your world. Some have gone into hiding, others have begun to steal, kill, and destroy. You have all been trained to find and annihilate the creatures and will continue to save your world."

"Lord, I want to save people from these monsters. I know I won't be able to go back to what I used to do anyway." Darrel shook his head. "That old life is over for me now." Darrel looked at each person. "And before we leave this place, I want to tell you all that I'm honored to have met you and made this journey with you."

They all gathered around and hugged him and laughed as they came away wearing some of Darrel's dirt and dust. Gianna wiped a tear from her eye as she pulled back and looked up at him.

"You're a good man, Darrel."

Darrel was speechless for a moment at Gianna's words. "Thanks, Gi. That really means a lot from you." He smiled.

"Really?"

"Yeah."

He rolled his eyes and adjusted an invisible tie. "I mean, I know you saw through my shiny exterior to the selfish jerk underneath."

They both laughed, and she nodded. "But, the change in you is apparent from the inside out." She got serious and looked up at him. "I see it. We all see it."

They all agreed with claps on the back and teary-eyes.

Jesus stepped up and embraced the dusty warrior. "Darrel, my son, you will lead armies." Darrel's mouth dropped open. The Lord grinned, then looked at all of them. "Each of you has gone through accelerated training in this realm and will lead many in a battle spanning multiple realms and spheres."

He then stepped in front of Diego, who bowed his head. "Diego, you have grown into a strong and even wiser leader. You have fathered so many over the years and have been faithful with what I have entrusted to your care. Look at me, my son." Diego looked up into Jesus' eyes. "I have healed your body."

"Thank...you, Lord," Diego said as he strained to hold

back his emotion.

The Lord shook His head and put his hand on Diego's face. "Surely, I bore your grief and carried your sorrows... even your sicknesses are mine, Diego. Now, I am giving you more revelation and wisdom, and you must write it all down and give it out in the time you have left, for it is still short."

Diego looked up questioningly. Jesus shook His head. "It is not for you to know now, my son. Only to redeem the time you have left."

"Yes, Master."

Yeshua stepped over to Lincoln, smiling wide, and Lincoln embraced him and began to weep. The Lord held him and spoke loving truths over him. "Lincoln, my son, my son. You are clean and whole! I have made all things new." The Lord held him for some time, and Gianna was moved by how tender and intentional the Master was to each one of them. After some time, Lincoln wiped his eyes and looked up at Jesus.

"Thank you, Lord . . ."

"Lincoln, you are a mighty warrior and monster slayer! You and Darrel will work together to lead armies."

Darrel slapped Lincoln on the back and put his arm around him.

The Lord moved on to Billie Jean, who instantly leaned her head on his chest. He stroked her hair and kissed the top of her head. "Who are you?" He whispered.

She pulled back, a flash of frustration hitting her chest, then she looked into the ocean of His eyes, in that very instant connecting to Spirit. "I am Your daughter. Your Beloved, and a mighty warrior." She beamed at Him because she genuinely believed it.

"Yes! Monster-slayer, Giant-killer...and the enemy will call you the sky-terror!" He laughed. "But most important..."

He whispered something in her ear; her mouth dropped open, and her eyes watered. He looked at her again, kissed her cheek, and stepped over to Lucy while everyone wondered what He said to her.

A tear slid down his cheek as He embraced Lucy, her head barely reaching His chest. "Ah, my sweet girl, it won't be easy for you to go back, I know." He looked into her eyes.

"Can she come home with me?" interjected Gianna.

Lucy looked at Gianna surprised, then back at Jesus with a hopeful expression.

"Daughter, you are stronger now than you ever were, and you know you are not alone, yes?"

She nodded.

"Right now, you are the only connection that your mother has to me. I long for her to come to me and be free from her shackles and pain."

Lucy nodded again. "Yes, Jesus. I do want you to help her get off drugs. I know she could be a good mom if she wasn't so messed up all the time, ya' know?"

He smiled and squeezed her hand. "Yes, I do know. And don't worry, I'll show you what to do and when."

"Okay, I'm good with that, but will I see Gianna again? And the others?"

"Yes, Daughter, you will be seeing a lot of each other from now on." He embraced her again and then turned to Gianna.

Gianna willed herself not to cry, which only resulted in her scrunching up her face like she smelled something bad, so she sniffled and tweaked her nose. He watched her with amusement for a moment.

"It's perfectly fine for you to cry too, My Love."

His words released the waterworks, and Gianna cried into his chest as he held her. When she was through and wiped her tears, she looked at him and sniffled. "Okay, I'm ready now."

"Gianna, I need you for a hard assignment."

"Yes, Lord, whatever you need me to do," she replied, willing to do whatever He asked at that moment.

"Amora. She has never known love. I would like you to make her a part of your family. Help her to heal, and train her to use her abilities to fight the enemy."

"Yes, Lord," she stammered. "I...I'm definitely willing. I just worry; with the state of my marriage, if we'll be able to show her a loving family life."

He pulled her into an embrace and whispered in her ear. "Daughter, I make all things new. I am healing all of you, and you need Amora as much as she needs you. All of you." He pulled back and looked into her eyes. "Will you take her and leave the rest of it to me?"

He didn't let her answer but addressed the group. "The entities that passed through the portals are a poison that must be eradicated. Their very physical presence makes the already dark world even darker. Think of it like a large cancer cell; we cut 98% of it off, but the 2% that's left has the potential to grow and devour."

Gianna pondered His question as she followed Him.

He was still instructing them as He began to guide them towards a red portal doorway. "Also, there are others."

"What, others?" Lincoln asked.

"Others that serve me and have special abilities. I've been warning them in dreams and visions to prepare. You will find them and make them a part of your team."

"How will we find them?" asked Darrel.

"They will find you."

Their minds were spinning, and they had a million questions.

"More instructions will come, my children."

CHAPTER 21

You will never escape! We will come for you, and we will kill you!

The demonic voice came from inside her head, and immediately, Amora felt hands around her throat, cutting off her air as she struggled to get free. Fear and panic quickly overtook her. She called out in her mind for the Man of Light to help her. Instantly, the hands were gone, and she could breathe. She shot up in bed, gasping for air, looking around for her attacker, but she only saw other sleeping children in beds around the room. Her heartbeat slowed. She got up to go to the bathroom and wondered if it was a nightmare.

As she walked, she saw a vision like a movie screen playing in front of her. In the vision, she saw her father. He was pinned down on his office desk by Lucifer, who had him by the throat.

"You let them take her, and now you will pay for your incompetence with your life!"

Her father squirmed, his eyes wide with fear, as his life slowly seeped away.

Satan threw his body to the side like a piece of trash, and then grabbed her mother and slammed her down, putting his face uncomfortably close to hers.

"You have one chance to make it up to me, Adora. If you please me, I will spare your life and allow you to take over leadership of this coven and take your husband's place on the Council."

Adora nodded vigorously.

"I may even forgive the fact that you were going to slay my bride without my permission when we already had a sacrifice in place."

He relaxed his grip slightly, so she could speak. "It was Viktor! He was afraid because she saw him! Jesus!"

Satan scowled. "Of course she did. Viktor was a fool. Amora has too much power and training to slay because of one encounter with the enemy."

Adora nodded again.

"You *will* find your eldest daughter and bring her back. She will become my bride, and I will assure her loyalty by filling her with the three wickedest entities in my kingdom, making her the most feared and powerful witch in the Brotherhood!"

The Waking

"Yes, I will find her!"

Amora saw three dark figures floating behind Satan as he spoke. Tall, thick muscled reptilian beings with yellow eyes and alligator shaped faces. They watched the scene with ravenous hunger. Lucifer ripped Adoras's clothes off and proceeded to brutally ravage her.

Amora turned away in revulsion as the scene faded. Immediately, a bright light filled the room, and indescribable peace came in, completely wiping out all fear from what she just witnessed. The Man of Light, Jesus, held her close, and she fell easily into His embrace.

Gianna woke at the sound of an alarm clock. The sound pulled her from a horrible nightmare of Satan brutalizing a blonde woman in an office. She reached over to her husband's side of the bed for comfort, but it was empty. Shaking her head, she chided herself, remembering he was still staying at his sister's home since they separated a month ago. She swung her legs to the floor and sat for a moment, rubbing her eyes as she tried to grasp reality.

Suddenly, she felt a cold shiver run down her spine and looked up. Out of the corner of her eye, Gianna saw something small and dark dart past her bedroom door, and her cat, Tigger, zoomed by in pursuit. She quickly followed, turning on lights along the way, and found the cat hissing at something he had blocked into a corner. She instinctively reached for her blade, which astonishingly appeared at her back as she grabbed for it.

Gianna caught the glint of a small blade as a minuscule grey-green creature came into view. She quickly pierced through the miniature goblin before it could stab Tigger with its tiny sword. A horrible odor emanated from the small monster as green goo poured out of its wound. Disgusted, she quickly opened a window and tossed the hideous little corpse into the back yard with her sword. Gianna wiped off her blade on her pajama pants and re-sheathed; it disappeared.

Before she had time to process what just happened, her doorbell rang. Her son, Dylan, emerged from his room, rubbing his eyes.

"Mom, who's at the door?"

She scooped him up and kissed his face, holding him close as she felt like it had been ages since she had seen him last. He wiggled free of her embrace. Since he had turned eight, he had become too old for that "mushy" stuff.

Gianna grabbed his hand, still cautious after the earlier

ordeal.

"Let's go see."

They went downstairs, and she cracked the front door; she caught her breath in surprise. There, on her porch, was Uriel, dressed inconspicuously in jeans and a t-shirt. Amora stood at his side, holding a duffel bag. They stepped in, and she looked out to see if anyone or "anything" saw them enter.

"Don't worry, we're cloaked," said Uriel rubbing his beard.

She nodded and then quickly shut and locked the door. She ran her hands through her messy hair. "So, this is really happening?"

Uriel raised his eyebrows at her.

"Can I get you some coffee?"

Dylan looked at the tall, muscular man and young blonde girl with curiosity. Amora approached the boy.

"Hi, I'm Amora, what's your name?

"I'm Dylan. You wanna come and see my new Lego set?"

"Sure."

She smiled and followed Dylan up the stairs.

EPILOGUE:

Lincoln and Darrel made sure to get a booth in the back of the dirty diner. They were told to be there at precisely 8pm but arrived a few minutes early, so they sat and ordered a pot of coffee.

"Do you think he'll show?"

Darrel added cream to his cup and looked around before answering. "This dude, Alvin, is the real deal, Link. I knew his brother when we were kids. He enlisted a few years ago, and nobody really heard from him after that. His brother said he stopped coming home because he couldn't talk about anything he was doing overseas. He felt like it was safer for everyone if he just didn't get tempted to talk. You know what I mean?"

He paused and looked around again.

No one in the place seemed interested in anything but their own plates. A couple of old guys sat at the front counter, some teenagers giggled in a booth up front, and a young couple nearby were more interested in their phones than each other.

Darrel seemed satisfied and continued, "He called me

out of the blue the other day and said he was told to contact me, that he could talk to me and I would know what to do. That was it; then he told me where to meet him."

Lincoln shook his head and was about to respond when a tall, well-built black man entered. He was dressed in jeans and a button-up dress shirt, but his face showed serious business, and his eyes were searching. Seeming to spot them, he headed their way, but before he sat down, he stopped.

"Darrel Coleman?"

Darrel started to stand up.

"Don't stand up."

The man sat down next to Lincoln, whose seat at the booth faced the front door. Alvin looked at Darrel for a moment before speaking.

"I had a dream about you. You were flying, lit up with fire, and you were fighting some of the same kinds of freakish creatures that my team has been taking down and collecting for the last few weeks."

Darrel nodded. "This is my friend, Lincoln. We both have experience with what you described. We need to know where you are finding them, so we can destroy them."

"Can you really do it? What I saw in my dream?"

Darrel put his hand on the table palm up to show a fireball appear in it. Quickly, he closed his fist, and it disappeared before anyone noticed. The soldier's eyes got big, then, just as quickly, went business again. He spoke low.

"My team is the best of the best, trained in every tactical and martial art, sent on the most secret missions to take out and, at times, bring back live specimens for the government to study and use. For years, we've dealt with things that only turned up in horror movies and nightmares, but only a few here and there actually came up as real creatures with no scientific explanation. That all changed a few weeks ago."

The solemn face began to weaken. Alvin looked down, rubbing his hand across his cheek to the back of his head. He looked up again, worry in his eyes.

"They've tried real hard to keep it all out of the media or change the stories, so people don't know what's really going on and cause a panic. That mass shooting in DC a couple weeks ago," he made finger quotations as he said mass shooting, "that was actually a three-headed dragon thing with a lion's body. It came out of the reflecting pool at the Washington monument, just started eating people, men women and children, it just tore them apart. . .”

Alvin paused and pressed both his palms to his eyes. “By the time we got there, it had devoured almost everyone nearby and a few police officers who had come on the scene. We finally took it out by slicing the heads off. A few of our guys actually carry swords because we’ve come to understand the nature of these beasts. Bullets don’t usually work. . . it was the worst thing I’d ever witnessed on a scene.”

He paused, closed his eyes, and whispered, “Blood and body parts everywhere, man! Kids, man!” Alvin looked up, and he was terrified, his eyes red with unshed tears.

Lincoln stroked his beard silently, his stomach in knots at the thought of the scene, but unfortunately, he had become familiar with similar sights as of late.

Alvin shook his head slowly and continued, “I just got back from Guatemala. We were tracking a pair of giants through the mountain areas of the Cuchumatanes. We got word that they had been there a couple of weeks, coming out of hiding in the forest every couple of days to feed. Turns out, they prefer human flesh, though we still found plenty of animal carcasses as well. These things definitely didn’t care if they left a trail. Our orders were to bring one back alive.”

Darrel and Lincoln exchanged looks.

Alvin nodded. "Believe me, it's worse than you think. That's why after years of keeping secrets, I'm done. I'm not keeping them anymore!"

He was a bit more worked up and forgot to keep his voice low. A few people turned their direction. Darrel put his hand on the man's arm. "Hey, Alvin, man. Calm down. We're here. We get you, okay?"

Alvin put his face in his hands and nodded. "Look, man, there were sixteen of us...only five came back alive."

He stopped again. "All because our government wants to turn soldiers into those...things!"

"Listen, Alvin." Lincoln moved his coffee to the side and looked the man in the eye. "I know you don't know us, and it took a lot for you to come here to meet a couple strangers, but I assure you, we absolutely believe you, and we want to help."

"Thank you, sir," Alvin responded, his face looking a bit more relaxed.

"Please, just call me Lincoln. What happened when you got back from that trip to Guatemala?"

Alvin rubbed the back of his head and sighed. "They

gave all the survivors vacation leave," he continued with a whisper, his voice cracking slightly. "They told us to go to the beach and relax for a few weeks, all expenses paid." He shook his head. "I just want to be on the right side of this, man! I know what's happening, and more people are going to die if we don't do something!"

Darrel nodded. "You did the right thing, Alvin. We have a team that's doing something, and we need you and any more that are willing to come on board."

Alvin nodded. "Who are you with?... And why did I dream about you?"

Darrel answered, "God."

AUTHOR BIO

Cheryl McClamrock and her husband have been married 21 years and are parents to three amazing, unique sons—their pride and joy! She is a busy, licensed Realtor, personal trainer, and new business owner of Snap Fitness in Missouri City, TX. Cheryl is a new author, a speaker and teacher, and an ordained minister, who plans on, with the Lord's help, continuing to publish new stories, books, and blogs.

Cheryl is enjoying life on the move! She loves hiking in national parks, fitness, bumming on the beach with a good book, and traveling. Most of all, Cheryl is a passionate lover of God. She lives to know Him and make Him known in all aspects of her varied and abundant life.

www.ingramcontent.com/pod-product-compliance
Lightning Source LLC
Chambersburg PA
CBHW060233100726
47907CB00003B/613